IN PURSUIT OF THE PAST

CAROLYN LAROCHE

HOT TREE PUBLISHING

ALSO BY CAROLYN LAROCHE

MARSHALL BROTHERS

Murder on the Mountain

Blue Ridge Murder

Danger on the Mountain

DEFENDERS OF LOVE

Witness Protection

Homeland Security

Border Patrol

STAND-ALONE

In Pursuit of the Past

IN PURSUIT OF THE PAST

CAROLYN LAROCHE

For information, contact the publisher, Hot Tree Publishing.

www.hottreepublishing.com

Editing: Hot Tree Editing

Cover Designer: BookSmith Design

E-book ISBN: 978-1-922679-45-1

Paperback ISBN: 978-1-922679-46-8

*For you, Dad. It feels like a lifetime ago
and yet no time at all since we lost you.
I hope I've made you proud.
Love you always.*

ONE

Feigning nonchalance, she glanced over her shoulder—and confirmed her fear. The black sedan with its darkly colored windows still followed her slowly through the center of town. The little hairs at the back of Ava's neck prickled, and adrenaline had her heart rate kicking up.

Catching a glimpse of the vehicle in a shop window, she picked up her pace. Tiny beads of sweat formed on her forehead and ran down the sides of her face. Gooseflesh prickled on her arms despite the warm summer morning.

The cemetery was still six blocks away. Plenty of time for her pursuers to do whatever it was they had planned to do to her. Ava scanned the length of the street ahead of her, looking for someone—anyone—

who might be able to help her. Being that it was barely half past six in the morning on a Sunday, the entire town was still sound asleep.

Well, everyone except for her and her scary secret admirer.

Walking as fast as possible without breaking into a full-on run, Ava made a direct beeline to the cemetery. As she moved faster, so did the car. Two blocks away from her destination, the driver of the car revved the engine. She passed a furtive glance back at the vehicle as her heart rate shifted into super high gear. Sweat dripped down her back as her mouth went dry. Glancing around for something to use to protect herself, Ava caught sight of a large tree branch that had fallen on the lawn in front of the library.

Changing her direction slightly, she ran toward the branch.

She heard the roar of the engine as the driver hit the gas pedal. Fairly certain they were going to follow her onto the lawn, Ava bypassed the branch and ran to the large front doors of the library. There was no way the car could get up there, although its driver definitely could. Panic began to strangle the air from her lungs.

As she bounded up the wide stone steps, the

whoop whoop of a police siren stopped her in her tracks.

A black-and-white SUV with the words Sunrise Police on the side pulled directly in front of the sedan. The other driver whipped the wheels to the right, spinning the vehicle in a semicircle and leaving black rubber tire tracks on the road.

"Thank God." Ava took several deep breaths as every muscle in her body began to quiver. The adrenaline that had coursed through her veins, giving her the speed to make it to the steps, flooded her cells. She dropped to the cool stone and continued to breathe deeply.

The police cruiser parked in front of the library. As the officer inside stepped out, Ava bit back a curse.

Hudson.

"What are you doing here?" she asked, definitely sounding more annoyed than grateful despite the fact that Hudson had probably just saved her from something awful.

He leveled an unemotional stare at her. "You really shouldn't be walking around out here alone at this hour, Ava. Bad things happen when you aren't paying attention. "

"It's six thirty in the morning, and the sun is shining. How awful could it be?"

Giving her a brief once-over, Hudson got back into his truck and drove away without saying another word.

Watching the taillights of his SUV grow smaller and smaller, Ava held a palm to her chest. She could still feel the pounding of her heart, but the cause had shifted some. Hudson's words stung, irritating a wound that had never quite healed.

Grasping the railing and pulling herself to her feet, Ava searched the street in an effort to convince herself the black car was truly gone. Satisfied the occupant had moved on, she continued on to her destination. Hudson's parting statement had struck a chord, making her more angry than grateful at his perfect timing.

As she walked, Ava definitely kept an eye out for the car, but there was no sign of it. Only once she made it safely inside the gates of the Sunrise Cemetery did she start to relax a little.

On this day of all the days in a year, she had to encounter Hudson, the one person she would prefer to avoid for the rest of her life. Yet there he was, showing up like a prince on a white steed, rescuing her when she wanted absolutely no rescuing or anything else from him. Showing up like that, despite the fact that it was perfect timing, irked her to no end.

Just another thing that was out of her control for Hudson to judge or hold against her.

"Ugh. Why did you have to be the one to show up?" She clenched her hands into fists, digging her fingernails into her palms to keep from screaming in frustration. Finally forcing Hudson from her thoughts, she strolled through the well-kept landscape until she found the headstone she wanted.

Ava sat cross-legged on the freshly mown grass in front of it. The delicate carving of a butterfly in the marble made her smile and want to cry at the same time, as it always did. Her best friend loved butterflies so much; she'd kept a monarch habitat and a butterfly garden since her sixth birthday.

For early morning, the ground and the air were surprisingly dry. She pulled the clip from her long hair, enjoying the lack of humidity. The panic-induced perspiration that covered her skin ten minutes earlier had dissipated. For the moment, anyway. By late morning, her curls would be plastered to her neck and forehead, but for now, she would bask in the gift of the pleasant weather.

The colors of the early morning sky didn't disappoint. "From God's hands to our eyes," her nana used to say. Of course, she did live in the town most known around the world for its beautiful sunrises, thus earning its name: Sunrise, North Carolina. The least inhabited and most beautiful stretch of land on the northern end of the barrier islands that made up the Outer Banks. A tourist destination for thousands, home to only a few hundred. Ava had grown up in Sunrise and returned after college. She couldn't imagine living anywhere else. Even after what had happened to Quinn.

Leaning back and resting her hands on the ground behind her, she looked up, searching for a sign from her friend. "Hey, girl. It's me." That was the same greeting she used to use every time she called or texted her best friend. It brought her comfort in its repetition.

Someone had left a fresh bouquet on Quinn's memorial. Without a body, there had been nothing to bury. Quinn's stubborn brother had insisted on the stone, though, positioned beside their parents. To Ava it felt like he'd given up hope on Quinn ever returning.

She sighed. Maybe Hudson was right. Maybe Ava had held on to an empty hope for so long. After so many years, though, it definitely helped to have somewhere to go to feel close to Quinn.

The circumstances surrounding her best friend's "death" had been sketchy, to say the least. Probably because Quinn wasn't actually dead. Ava had insisted for months that there was no way Quinn could have gone under the waves. She was far too good a swimmer. Not that anyone would listen to her about that. Not the cops, and definitely not Quinn's bullheaded brother. Eventually, Ava gave up trying to make people believe her and let her public proclamations rest. If Quinn wasn't dead and wanted to be found, she would have been. That's what everyone told her.

She sighed, enjoying the peace of the cemetery. This was as close as she could get to her best friend, so she made do with what she had.

Talking to Quinn had always given her perspective, and she seemed to need it way more often than she used to. Especially on this particular day.

She straightened the steel stand that held the most recent offering in her best friend's memory as she remained seated on the soft grass

Heaven had always been something Ava believed in, but Quinn had plenty of questions about God and Heaven. Ava preferred to entertain the thought that her best friend had secured a spot if she had indeed met with St. Peter at the Pearly Gates. So, for the moment, she visited the only place that felt connected to Quinn, whether she was dead or alive.

A light breeze ruffled her curls. Maybe it was Quinn's way of letting her know she was there.

"I miss ya, you know. Things around here have never quite been the same. Your brother has never been the same either. I keep hoping one day he'll realize he doesn't have to keep punishing himself, but you know him—stubborn as a mule."

She left out the part about Quinn's brother punishing *her* for the last decade. Her friend didn't need that detail just yet.

Ava ran her fingertips across the surface of the grass. The movement felt soothing to the very rough emotions she still carried with her. After what happened that morning and then this being *the* day, her heart was raw.

A loud chirp sounded from a nearby tree. A brilliant red cardinal sat there, perched on the branch closest to her.

She laughed. "I knew you would be around today. Thank you for showing up."

The cardinal chirped animatedly, making Ava laugh even more.

For the second time that morning, the little hairs along the back of her neck stood at attention. Had the person in the dark sedan found her? She sat up straight, scanning the memorial garden, unable to shake the feeling of being watched. A bit of movement caught her attention. Ava stood up.

Glancing around for an escape route and finding nothing promising, she steeled her nerves and announced in what she hoped was a forceful tone, "You might as well show yourself. I know you're there."

Ava held her breath, feeling completely exposed in the empty cemetery. She took a deep, nerve-steadying inhale, praying that whoever it was, it wasn't the pursuer from earlier.

A man stepped into view, his familiar form causing an instant knot to form in her stomach. The way his broad shoulders filled out the Sunrise police uniform he wore was a stark contrast to the lanky, almost skinny teenager he'd once been.

"Again, Hudson?"

He didn't reply, just looked past her at Quinn's headstone.

She tried again. "Are you intentionally following me for some reason today?"

She'd really hoped to avoid him at this place in particular. Even more so after his ice-cold attitude just thirty minutes earlier.

He averted his gaze from the headstone and

looked at her, disapproval darkening his eyes, but again didn't say anything, frustrating her even more.

"I didn't realize you'd be here so early, since you're working. I would have waited until after church."

"It's just a bird, you know." He motioned to the tree. "Cardinals are everywhere around here."

"I like to think a cardinal represents a visit from a loved one. In this case, a visit from Quinn." Ava blew a little kiss to the bird. "Love you, girl."

The cardinal flew off, leaving her alone with the one man she'd really hoped *not* to run into that day. And now she'd done so *twice*.

Hudson rolled his eyes. "That's ridiculous."

"Maybe to you, since you seem to have lost your belief in a lot of things, but not to me. Quinn gave me a suncatcher when we were kids. It says, 'When cardinals appear, angels are near.' It's a comforting thought. It's like the cardinal is her own personal messenger from wherever she is." Ava had absolutely no idea why she brought that up. Just like when they were kids, Hudson's presence had her all off-kilter, making her babble. Only now, the reasons were far more complicated than a childhood crush.

He leaned against the trunk of the tree the cardinal had been hanging out in. "Quinn was a dreamer. If she'd been more focused—"

"There is nothing wrong with having dreams." Ava felt the moisture well up in her eyes, forcing her to look away from Hudson. It had been exactly one year since they'd had this same kind of conversation. A strained, formal chat where once they had been so comfortable with each other. She had far easier interactions with the checkout people at the supermarket. A stranger looking in wouldn't have begun to guess Ava and Hudson had known each other their entire lives.

"She got it from our father. If he hadn't been such a dreamer, searching for buried treasure in the ocean, that hurricane wouldn't have killed both our parents." He rolled and unrolled the baseball-style cap he held as he, too, avoided eye contact. "I didn't expect to see you here either. It's awfully early."

Ava felt a little flutter in her chest. She hated her stupid heart for its betrayal. After ten years, Hudson ought to be a stranger to her. At the very least, she should be angry at him. Instead, his presence felt a little like home. Another thing she hated her traitorous heart for. After so many years, she should have gotten way over any feelings she'd ever had for Hudson Pierce.

She shrugged. "I like to come here and talk to her.

She'll always be my best friend, no matter how you feel about it."

"People might think you're a little crazy, sitting in a cemetery, talking to a dead person."

She shrugged again. "I don't think she's dead. I just have nowhere else to go when I want to feel close to her. You made sure of that."

Hudson narrowed his eyes at her as though deciding if her little jab was worth a response. Finally, he just grunted. "I'll come back later."

Ava'd had about enough of his grumpy mountain-man attitude. "No. Stay. I'm headed to church anyway. Don't let me stop you from being angry at the world."

He grunted again. "Church? How's that working out for you?"

She rested her hands on her hips and stared him down. "I have no idea what that's supposed to mean."

"God has quite the sense of humor, taking my parents and then my sister the exact same way, just a few years from each other. I don't trust the old geezer anymore. Haven't for years."

"You are a very angry man. Maybe Quinn would have come home by now if you'd had a little faith."

"Quinn's dead. All the faith in the world isn't going to bring her back."

The coldness to his words pierced her like a knife.

A cloud passed in front of the early morning sun, casting a shadow over them. They stood there, eyeing each other, each one daring the other to say what they really wanted to.

"It's obvious that's really what you choose to believe. I'm not going to try and change your mind anymore. That ship has sailed, and I am done chasing after it." She turned and walked away, feeling the heat of his glare all the way out of the cemetery.

"You need to let her go, Ava," Hudson called after her. "It's been ten years. Don't you think we would have heard something by now if she were alive?"

She stopped walking, turning to look back at Hudson. His broken expression stabbed her hard in the chest. "I will never let her go. Just like I could never let you go if you were the one who had disappeared. Quinn was the sister I never had. Her memory, at the very least, will always live on with me."

He shrugged. "Suit yourself. And watch your back. I saw that same sedan parked down the block when I pulled in. They drove off as soon as I drove up in front of the gate."

A slight chill ran through her. Why would anyone be following her? "I'll be fine, but thanks for the warning."

Hudson didn't reply. Instead, he turned his back on her and moved closer to the graves of his family.

Ava walked faster than usual to cover the short distance between the cemetery and the church. Doing her best not to think about all that was, or what would never be, she forced Hudson from her mind, replacing him with memories of her childhood and Quinn. This day should only be about her best friend.

It only took a few minutes to walk to the little white church in the center of town. With no sign of her mysterious stalker, she relaxed. Church members milled around, chatting on the entrance steps and in the large vestibule inside. Ava smiled politely as she passed through, said a few hellos, and went to sit in her usual spot.

Since her run-in with Hudson and the mysterious stalker got her adrenaline going, she felt fidgety and uneasy at church. At least six different scents of Sunday-only perfume surrounded her, the warmth in the space intensifying the headache she had building from the assault on her sense of smell. Every so often she'd begin the head-bob-eye-droop process, only to jerk awake as Pastor Barrett pounded the pulpit or addressed the congregation.

"Take care of the widows!" Pastor Barrett called out. "Love the orphans as your own!"

Murmured prayers of "Amen" sounded all around her. Ava settled back against the wooden pew, trying to focus on the sermon and how she could apply it to her own mission as an adoption worker. She'd made it her life's work to love the orphans. And the abandoned, abused, and otherwise unwanted children. One day, maybe, she'd finally be able to forgive herself for any part she had in her friend's disappearance—once she righted enough wrongs to balance the one wrong she could never fix.

"Oh good Lord!" one of the older ladies in the congregation cried out. "Stop the sermon!"

Pastor Barrett chuckled. "Is it too much for you to handle today, Ms. Freya?"

Ripples of laughter passed through the sanctuary.

Ava turned to look at the woman well-known for her exuberant clothing and dramatic ways. The brightly colored dress she'd donned for church that day did not disappoint. Standing by the main entrance to the old country church, she fanned herself with an oversized straw hat. The woman's face had flushed an unhealthy red color. "I think your message today may have been too powerful!"

Pastor Barrett didn't even try to hide his concern when he asked, "Ms. Freya, do you need me to call an ambulance? Is it your heart?" He already had his cell phone out of his pocket, ready to dial.

She laughed, a loud, nervous cackle. "Oh goodness, no! My heart is just fine. Well, mostly, anyway. It did just experience quite a shock, though."

Now the pastor just looked as confused as Ava felt. "Well, then, what's so wrong that you need me to stop preaching?"

"I'll show you." Freya dropped the hat and leaned down. When she stood back up, she held a tiny bundle wrapped in a blue blanket, stiff-armed in front of her as though the tiny human could somehow hurt her.

A shrill cry filled the sanctuary as everyone froze. Aside from the sobs of the child, no one said or did anything for a full twenty seconds. As miserable and uncomfortable as she looked, it was clear the woman had obviously never had any children or grandchildren.

"Where did that baby come from?" someone asked.

Freya pointed to the lobby through the doors behind her. "Out there. I went to, um, powder my nose and found the basket just sitting there in the middle of the room."

As if hit with a stroke of genius, Freya strode

down the center aisle, still holding the baby in front of her like she would a venomous snake. Stopping at the end of the row, she leaned forward and, holding the baby so close to Ava that she could smell baby powder, said, "You take this thing. You're the expert, after all."

Pastor Barrett stepped down off the pulpit, his eyes on Freya as he dialed that emergency number on his cell phone after all.

Still in a bit of shock, Ava rose from her seat and faced the older woman. "What should I do with him, Ms. Freya?"

Freya huffed. "How should I know? Isn't this your job? To take care of abandoned kids?"

Ava breathed deeply before speaking. She should just take the baby, and she would, but the woman's attitude added to her already sour mood. "My job is to find homes and families for children in need. Permanent homes. This is the police department's job."

The baby let out another scream, shocking Freya so much that her head jerked back, and she stumbled. Ava grabbed for the baby as the other woman tumbled to the ground, catching him just as Freya let go. Much to her surprise, he quieted down immediately. Grabbing a handful of Ava's thick hair, he leaned against her shoulder, making sweet little baby noises.

Her mood changed instantly. Something about the baby felt like he belonged right where he was.

"See?" Freya waved a hand at Ava from her position on the floor. "It's her job. Even the whipper-snapper knows it."

"I've called the police." Pastor Barrett returned his phone to his pocket. "He does seem quite settled with you, Ava. Would you mind holding him until the authorities get here?"

"Of course not, Pastor."

He turned his attention to the parishioner on the floor. "Are you okay, Ms. Freya?" He held out a hand to assist her up, but the woman waved it away with a grunt.

"I'm fine. Stop fussing over me, everyone!" She clumsily pulled herself to her feet, yanking her colorful dress back down over her ample backside.

Ava stepped out into the aisle and strode to the heavy wooden doors at the back of the chapel. Several folks milled around, gossiping about who could have possibly left the baby there. On a bench in the foyer sat a laundry basket. Tucked inside were several diapers, a can of powdered baby formula, and a couple bottles. Ava reached in and pulled up the blanket on the bottom to find several folded articles of clothing and a piece of paper.

"Someone must have been really moved by the pastor's sermon today." There were a few chuckles at the so-not-funny comment made by a man she didn't recognize. Most people didn't understand that what had happened was more than likely an act of love, but she'd been in her job long enough to recognize how difficult the decision had to have been for the unknown mother.

"If y'all want to go back in and listen to the rest, I'll wait out here for the police," Ava said, praying they would agree to do so. She sent a pleading look to the pastor, who'd just joined them.

He nodded and started herding people back inside. "Y'all need to hear my big finish. How about we get back to it?"

"What about the baby?" someone asked.

"As Ms. Freya said, Ava is very capable of handling this situation." He nodded in her direction. "If you need me, just peek in and wave."

"Thank you, Pastor."

Ava waited until the entry area was empty before sitting on the bench beside the baby basket. "Let's see if this note says anything about who would leave you here, little guy."

The baby let out a tiny sigh. He seemed completely calm with her. Ava often had that effect on infants and children. Just another reason why she was perfect for her job.

She unfolded the note, then smoothed it enough to read the neatly printed words.

> Please take good care of little Elijah. I call him Eli.
> Knowing he's in the one place I always felt loved gives me peace.
> Love him. Keep him safe. Please.
> When he gets older, tell him his mama loves him and will always be his RoD BFF, even if she's no longer here to tell him.

Ava gasped. *RoD BFF.* Ride or die, best friend forever.

The sheet of paper fell to the floor. She jumped up and ran outside, the baby still in her arms. *RoD BFF.* Only one person Ava knew had ever signed notes that way. She took the stone steps faster than she should and ran to the parking lot beside the church, searching the lot for anyone or any unfamiliar vehicle. She turned and ran back toward the church but continued to the corner of the block and looked around. Ava's pulse pounded loudly in her ears as she scanned the area.

Please, let it be true.

Sadly, the streets were empty.

Ava stood there for several minutes, letting her heart rate calm itself as she listed all the reasons why there was no way that note could have been from her long-lost best friend. A light breeze stirred her hair as Eli drifted off to sleep, his cheek pressed against her chest. Her pulse settled as the adrenaline dump cleared from her system. Feeling a bit shaky, Ava made her way back to the stone steps.

She still couldn't call the disappearance what the police had—death by drowning. Quinn was far too strong a swimmer who had years' worth of ribbons and records to prove it. Like her and Hudson, Quinn knew how to escape a rip current. Drowning wasn't something she'd have allowed, not as stubborn as her best friend had been.

Had been?

Still was?

Was someone playing a horrible trick on her? On this of all days?

"I sure hope you have a plan for this one, Lord. This little guy needs his mama, and if that note means anything, I'd really like my best friend back. Please." Since it was Sunday, and she'd actually attended most of the church service, Ava felt justified in making the small request.

She turned and headed back to the church. Down the block, she saw a Sunrise Police Department SUV slowing down in front of the old building.

Please don't let it be him. I can't do that three times in one day.

The SUV stopped in front of the church, and, of course, Hudson stepped out. Apparently, some prayers were not meant to be answered.

IN A SMALL TOWN LIKE SUNRISE, IT WASN'T every day that they got a call about an abandoned baby. Not even every year. In fact, nothing ever really happened in the sleepy coastal North Carolina town with its single stoplight and half a dozen businesses. It might even be fair to say that two of the most notable Sunrise events of his lifetime would be the death of his parents and Quinn's drowning. His job had been a lot less exciting than he'd expected it to be when he signed on to the police department eight years ago. An occasional domestic dispute or a fight at a bar between tourists visiting the small destination town were all they ever handled.

Hudson Pierce pulled his patrol unit up in front of the single nondenominational church in town. At least the person, whoever she was, had chosen a safe place to leave her child. Not that he expected God would protect it or anything like that, but he knew most of the people who made up the congregation would take good care of a baby.

When he was a rookie, he'd once found the remains of a deceased toddler who had wandered away from his tourist parents, and the image of blue, lifeless eyes surrounded by blond curls had never left his mind. That was the last missing child call he'd attended. Thankfully, this one sounded to be alive and well. Just abandoned.

A woman carrying an infant walked toward the church from the opposite direction. His gut clenched when he realized who it was.

Why her?

Two times in one year was too much for his heart to bear, but three times in the same morning? His emotions definitely couldn't handle that. Not on that particular day.

It was obvious from her expression that Ava felt the same way he did.

She spoke first, clutching the baby and its blanket close, like a shield between them. "Hudson. I'm sorry. I didn't know... well, you know...."

He grunted, then scowled. "We live in a really small town, so it's not like there are lot of cops to choose from on a Sunday morning."

"Yeah." She glanced around, avoiding looking at him. "Still, I didn't think it'd be you, or I would have let someone else wait with this little man."

"Don't worry about it." The hard edge to his voice warned her to let it go. Fortunately, she took his hint.

"So, someone left this baby in the lobby of the church this morning."

He raised an eyebrow. "I kinda figured, since that's what the 9-1-1 call said."

She frowned at him. "Can you stop acting like a giant jerk for a few minutes? This is serious. Someone abandoned their baby!"

It irritated him that she confronted him like that. Name-calling, of all things. Hudson hiked up his duty belt, a nervous habit he employed when he needed a second to think. Finally, he exhaled, no snarky reply coming to him. He decided on a *just the facts, ma'am* approach. "Just tell me what happened."

Her shoulders visibly relaxed some. "Pastor Barrett was talking about widows and orphans. Ms. Freya left the sanctuary and came back, stopping the sermon. When the pastor asked if everything was okay, she held up a baby. Then the baby cried, and she gave it to me. You know, because it's what I do. Anyway—"

He raised a hand to stop her. "So, she just found a random little kid lying on the floor?"

"Of course not." Ava turned and jogged up the steps.

Following her, he tried to ignore the annoying little tug in his chest every time she looked back at him. The physical response was a complete betrayal of his anger toward her. Not bothering to hold the door for him, Ava disappeared inside the church.

The heavy door creaked as he pulled it open. Strains of some hymn he vaguely recognized from a childhood of Sunday services with his parents echoed quietly in the entryway.

Ava was just standing up after grabbing something off the floor. She motioned him over to where she stood beside a bench. On the seat, there sat a white plastic laundry basket full of baby paraphernalia.

"He was in this. Whoever left him wanted him to

be well cared for. They obviously love him very much."

Hudson frowned as he looked through the contents of the basket. "Someone who loves their child doesn't abandon them like this in a building full of strangers."

Ava turned on him, anger darkening the green eyes he used to dream about. "*Or* she loves him very much and knew she couldn't do right by him. A good mother will do anything to keep her child safe. It's what people who love each other do. They don't just shove them away and pretend they don't exist."

It was obvious she no longer meant the baby. "Look, Ava, this is not the time or place—"

"To do what?" She raised an eyebrow. "Speak truth? That's what church is all about. The truth."

She obviously had plenty of her own anger, which was directed 100 percent at him. Not that she didn't have every right to be angry. He'd failed to keep his sister safe and had hurt Ava in the process.

Something suddenly occurred to him. "Why did you choose that word?"

"What word?" Ava busied herself making the basket into a bed once more. "Truth?"

"*Safe.* Why did you say a mother will do anything to keep their child *safe*?"

She set the baby in the basket and tucked his blanket in around him. The little guy shoved a fist in his mouth and sucked on it, his eyelids fluttering closed.

Quietly, she replied, "I just have a feeling there is more to this story than a simple baby drop-off. That's all."

She knew something she wasn't sharing with him. He'd always been able to read Ava like a book. As they stood there, neither one speaking, he weighed his chances of getting her to tell him what she was holding back.

Just as he'd settled on slim to none, the doors to the sanctuary opened, and churchgoers began to file out into the lobby.

"Oh thank the good Lord!"

Both Hudson and Ava turned to look at the loud woman coming toward them. He glanced back at Ava, raising one eyebrow in question.

Ava held a finger to her lips and pointed to the sleeping baby, quieting the woman down instantly. "Ms. Freya, this is Officer Pierce. He's here for the baby."

"Actually, I'm Detective Pierce." Hudson gave the woman a nod.

"Hmpf." Freya crossed her arms over her chest. "Detectives don't wear uniforms like that."

"I just happened to be covering for someone this morning when the call came in." He didn't mention that he always preferred to work on this particular day so he couldn't have much time to think. He didn't need Ava to know that. Pulling a little notebook and pen from his chest pocket, he made a couple notes about the baby. "Ms. Taft says you were the one to find the baby?"

"It was like the Lord wanted me to be the one." Freya fanned herself with her ridiculously large hat.

"I see." Hudson made another note on his pad. "And what makes you think that?"

Freya stared at him, obviously miffed by his question. "Because I am a good Christian woman, of course."

Hudson happened to glance at Ava just in time to see her roll her eyes. Some things hadn't changed, apparently. She'd done the same to him plenty of times in the past. Holding back a chuckle, he kept his expression stern. "Yes, of course. Did you happen to see who left the baby here?"

This time the older woman was the one to roll her eyes. "Don't you think I would have stopped her if I had?"

"Not if it meant you couldn't be the center of attention." Ava's words were quiet, meant only for herself, but he heard her. The Ava he'd once known would have gotten right in the lady's face and said those things, not murmured them to herself. Maybe some things had stayed the same, but apparently he wasn't the only one who had gotten a little more jaded.

Hudson closed his notebook and returned it to his pocket, along with the pen. "Thank you very much, ma'am. I'm sure God is impressed with your charitable efforts here today."

Freya looked like she wanted to say something else, but the pastor appeared and clapped Hudson on the shoulder. "Thanks for coming out here, son. This is a new one, even for an old dog like me."

"Just doing my job, sir. I've got to notify Child Protective Services so they can come and get the boy." Hudson pulled his phone from his pants pocket and hit the preprogrammed number as he walked away from the little group. He needed space. Like real space, not just a couple steps, between him and Ava. His emotions had barely survived their early morning meetups. This newest encounter had pushed him to his limits.

He could feel her watching him as he spoke to

one of the social services employees. If he could just keep his distance until the caseworker arrived, he'd be fine. Maybe he'd just tell Ava she had to leave. Which wouldn't work either, since the caseworker would want to talk to her.

You're a professional, man. You need to do your job. Just treat her like you would anyone else.

Sadly, his little pep talk fell short when Ava walked toward him. He considered bolting out the doors to wait in his patrol unit until Child Protective Services arrived, but that would leave the baby outside his watchful presence. That could mean a lot of trouble with the lieutenant.

Ava smiled at him. The kind of smile shared between strangers. It seemed she'd forgotten everything that had happened just an hour or so ago. "Were you able to get a hold of someone? It's Sunday, so sometimes it's tough to get a live person to answer the phone."

Hudson tapped his phone. "Got them on the first try. Apparently, she's just a block away. Once you're interviewed, you can go on and leave. They'll take good care of the little guy."

Her smile turned to a frown that created a little furrow between her eyebrows. At one time, he might have reached over and rubbed those lines away with his thumb. Instead, he shoved his hands into his pockets.

"I don't want them to put him in a foster home."

"Come on, Ava. You know how this works. You're part of the system too."

The doors to the church opened and then closed, letting in a warm breeze full of the promise of beach days and bonfire nights. Neither of which interested him anymore.

Those days were long gone.

All he could focus on at the moment was ending this interaction with Ava, getting through the rest of the day, and climbing back into his safe little shell of work and home. No complications and no darned emotions.

The doors to the church opened again, and a middle-aged woman wearing a dark suit and sunglasses entered the lobby.

"Detective Pierce?" she asked, looking toward him.

He gave her a nod, holding up a finger to let her know he'd be right over.

"Excuse me, Ava." Never so grateful for a distraction, he left Ava standing alone and joined the caseworker.

"I'm Janet James from CPS." The woman looked

around the room before her gaze settled on the laundry basket. "Is the baby in there?"

"Yes," he replied. "One of the churchgoers happened to find it during the church service."

"I'll need to speak to her and anyone else who might be helpful." Moving through the small crowd that still lingered, Hudson led her to the baby. The little boy slept soundly even with all the activity around him.

Out of the corner of his eye, he saw Ava slip out the front doors. He probably should have stopped her, since he knew Janet would want to interview her, but if he were being completely honest with himself, he didn't want to. If Janet did her job correctly, she'd find Ava on her own.

TWO

Her dress clung to her skin, the thin material thoroughly soaked from the thick humidity in the air by the time she made it to the end of her street. Such a change from just a couple hours ago. The ominous, dark clouds beginning to fill the sky definitely indicated a storm moving in off the ocean. Coastal storms hit hard and fast.

As if to prove that point, a heavy gust of wind caught the hem of her dress and whipped it around her legs. The damp fabric twisted and snapped. She really needed a cool shower and a change of clothes.

Ava picked up her pace, hoping she wouldn't turn an ankle in her sandals. If she'd known she'd need to escape so quickly, she'd have taken her car that day instead of walking the few blocks to the cemetery and then to the church. Seeing Hudson not once, not twice, but *three* times had really thrown her off-kilter, especially on the anniversary of the worst day of her entire life. And now a coastal storm would be like spoiled icing on a very nasty-tasting cake.

Making it into the house just as a few fat drops of water fell from the sky, Ava closed and locked the front door. Her near future definitely held a cool shower and some fresh clothes. She headed to the bathroom, holding her heavy, damp hair off her neck. The strands had frizzed up completely, giving her the look of someone who'd had an unfortunate run-in with an electric shock.

A loud crack of thunder sounded just as she reached in to turn on the water. Her mother had always said never to take a shower or bath in a storm. Whether it was true or not, Ava still didn't know. She sighed heavily as she turned the water back off and headed to her bedroom, her mother's words echoing in her head.

After switching on the ceiling fan, she flopped onto her back on the queen-sized bed just as another loud crack sounded. The skies opened up and let go of all the water they'd been holding on to at once. The room darkened as the wind whipped, and several more rounds of thunder and lightning passed overhead. The breeze created by the fan cooled her hot skin but made the wet dress even more uncomfortable.

Standing up, she pulled the sticky material over her head and tossed it onto the edge of the hamper. The note from the baby basket slipped out of one of the pockets. She scooped it up and set it on top of the comforter. After pulling on a pair of shorts and a T-shirt, she flopped back down onto the bed under the fan. Listening to the storm amp up, Ava considered the run-ins she'd had with Hudson and the note. She'd snatched it off the floor of the church and shoved it into her pocket before Hudson could see it. Technically, the note was evidence. Keeping it could get her in a lot of trouble. The legal kind. She should have given it to Hudson immediately. She just couldn't bring herself to do it.

For some reason, the urge to hold on to it was stronger than what she knew to be the right thing to do. That note might be a connection to her best friend. Parting with it felt like breaking a confidence.

RoD BFF.

That had to be Quinn. She couldn't imagine a single other person using that same abbreviation.

She sighed. Maybe it was a popular expression now. Ava had certainly fallen out of touch in many ways. Maybe Quinn had started a movement. Ava giggled at the thought. Quinn had certainly been a trendsetter in high school. Maybe it had carried over.

She rolled over onto her stomach, hugging a butterfly shaped pillow—a gift from Quinn a long time ago. Even after ten years, the ache in her heart still hadn't dulled.

Something crashed outside her window. Ava groaned. Her money was on the trash can that probably wasn't full anymore.

Hudson had taken Quinn's disappearance *really* hard and had never actually gotten over it. He blamed Ava, himself, the lifeguards, and pretty much everyone on the beach that day. If the note provided a clue as to where Quinn had been for so long, Ava felt like she owed it to Hudson to figure it out.

Maybe she'd take it to her office, make a photocopy, and then drop it by the police station, telling him she'd forgotten it was in her pocket. Once the storm passed, of course.

Another crash of thunder followed almost instantly by a flash of lightning had her heart pounding against her sternum. The electricity blinked off, then back on. Ava rolled onto her side to plug her cell phone into the bedside charger. Might as well get as much juice in the battery as she could in case the power went out. As she rolled herself back into place, she heard paper crinkle.

She felt around the bed for the note. If this really was from her long-lost best friend, she owed it to her to try and find her. Ignoring the fact that it was Hudson's actual job to do that very thing, she smoothed the piece of paper and ran her fingers over the script. It was familiar and yet different. Not nearly as neat and pretty as Quinn's writing had been when they were kids. This single sheet of paper gave her hope. It proved to her what she'd always known. Her best friend, and Hudson's only sister, had to be alive —and this letter confirmed it. At least to her. If she could just figure out how to prove it.

Grabbing her phone, she snapped a photo of the letter. Easier than trudging into the office to copy it. Eventually, sooner rather than later, she'd have to confess to Hudson and turn the page over to him. No one said she had to delete the picture, though. After the storm, she'd still run to work and make a photocopy of it. The picture was just extra insurance.

The sound of smashing glass had her jumping off the bed and running toward the front room of her tiny beach cottage. The large bay window that she loved so much lay in a hundred pieces on the hardwood floor of the living room. Several of the plants that had sat on a table in front of the window were scattered on the floor as well, dirt and broken pottery everywhere. The wind whipped rain and debris into her home, creating muddy rivers with the potting soil.

A giant rock sat in the center of the rain-soaked space. It had two words spray-painted in black across its surface.

WE KNOW.

She ran to the front door and yanked it open in time to hear tires squealing down the block. However, the rain blocked her view of anything except a pair of red taillights disappearing down the street.

Ava slammed the door shut against the storm—not that it mattered now that the storm filled her living room. *WE KNOW.* The message was brief and could mean a million things. After all, she worked for an agency that had placed a lot of babies. Her gut told her it had to do with Eli, though. Quinn's message had said the baby was in danger.

There was only one thing she could do. Someone had just thrown a small boulder through her window in a crazy thunderstorm. Someone else had left a baby in the church. A man had followed her through town early in the morning. The three things had to be related. Ava felt it in her gut: this was bigger than an unhappy birth parent mourning an adoption. And for some reason, she was being placed in the middle of it. There was no longer any choice but to call for help.

Running to her bedroom to grab her cell phone off the charger, Ava then searched for Hudson's phone number. She'd never deleted it, couldn't bring herself to do it. Just as she found it, the lights went out. Whatever had taken down the electricity had also knocked out cell service, judging by the missing bars on the phone screen.

If the storm didn't stop soon, her cottage would become an ark. The streets were probably flooded, making it way too dangerous to try driving at the moment.

A bolt of lightning lit up her bedroom. The accompanying boom pounded in her chest. Locking herself in the bathroom, Ava climbed into the tub to wait out the rest of the storm. Between the wind and rain, a waterspout coming onto shore wouldn't surprise her. Even a small tornado would take out her tiny house.

After what seemed like forever, the rain finally stopped, and the winds slowed. As blue skies became visible through the tiny bathroom window once more, Ava got up and stepped out of the bathtub.

A flick of the light switch confirmed the power had not come back on. Her cell phone proved to be equally useless. She left the bathroom, grabbed her purse off her dresser, and dropped the note she had put back in her pocket into it along with the useless cell phone, hoping service would return soon. Hudson should be at the police station. At least, she hoped so. As much as she dreaded it, she knew she had to hand over the note and tell him about the mess in her living room.

Stopping only to slip on tennis shoes and, at the last moment, take her phone back out to snap a quick photo of the words on the rock before returning it to her bag, Ava pulled open the front door, intending to try to drive to the police department. The giant piece of tree lying over the top of her sedan changed her plans.

Looking skyward, she sighed heavily. "Is there anything else you'd like to toss out here today? My living room is flooded, the car is probably totaled, and there's a note in my purse from a presumed dead woman."

A bright red cardinal flew past her head and

perched on the downed tree, chirping like crazy at her.

Some kind of sign? She sure hoped it meant going to Hudson was the right thing to do.

The street in front of her house was littered with debris. Leaves, branches, and even some sand filled the drains along the edges of the streets. A few houses down from hers, she spotted the reason for the power outage—a giant limb tangled in the lower lines, sparks shooting out of the mess every so often.

With no car, options were limited. She sighed, knowing she had no other choice. "I guess it's a good day for another walk."

Ava slowly picked her way through debris and around standing water and began the trek to the police station.

HUDSON HAD LONG SINCE DITCHED THE polyester uniform and changed into street clothes. He now sat at his desk in the office he shared with four other detectives. A sharp rap on the door pulled his attention from the report he'd been writing about the abandoned baby.

"Come in."

One of the young patrol officers pushed the door open. "Hey, Pierce, you got a visitor."

"I'm off the clock. Tell them to leave a message at the desk." He turned his attention back to the report, dismissing the interruption.

"Hud, she's insistent on seeing you. Says it's about someone named Quinn."

Hearing his sister's name, Hudson froze. It could only be one person wanting to see him, and he absolutely wasn't prepared to see Ava Taft four times in one day.

"Excuse me, I got this. Thank you for your help." Ava stepped around the officer and closed the door in his face.

Hudson stood up at his desk, secretly amused that the Ava he remembered had just made an appearance. The Ava who didn't let anyone tell her what to do. He kept his expression stern, despite the uptick in his pulse at her arrival. "You aren't supposed to be back here."

"Yeah, well, I knew you'd never talk to me otherwise."

He took in her disheveled appearance. The shorts and shirt she wore were streaked with water and dirt. Heavy waves of hair hung in wet clumps around her shoulders, and her bright green eyes seemed a little wild. Her hands shook as she stood there, eyeing him with agitation.

"What's so important you had to run here in a storm and barge into an off-limits area?" He narrowed his eyes and frowned. "I could arrest you for that, you know."

"Add it to the list, then." Ava dropped down into a chair in front of his desk.

"What list? What are you talking about?" She had him all sorts of confused.

"I didn't run here through the storm, you fool. Although, the way my heart is racing, I feel like I did."

Hudson leaned back in his chair. "Then why do you look like you went three rounds with an angry sea turtle?"

"An angry sea turtle? I don't think they even *get* angry! Why are you so ridiculous?" She dug into her purse and took out her cell phone. After pulling something up on the screen, she handed it to him. "That's why I'm wet."

Hudson accepted the phone and studied the picture on the screen. A large rock with the words *WE KNOW* painted across it sat in the middle of a trashed room.

He looked up at her. "Where did you find this?"

"On the floor of my living room after it smashed

through my bay window. All the water you see? That's from the storm invading my home, and it's also the reason I look like this." She gestured up and down the length of her form.

"Ava, why would you come to me with this?" He handed the phone back to her. "Why not just call 9-1-1 and make a report?"

She dropped the phone back into her purse and pulled out a piece of paper. "Well, for one thing, I had no cell service at the time. And also because I'm pretty sure it has something to do with this." She handed him the paper.

Hudson set the wrinkled, water-stained sheet on his desk and read the note, his heart rate speeding up with every word. By the time he made it to the end, his pulse pounded so loudly in his ears that everything else around him faded away. Picking it up, he read the whole thing again. And then once more, just in case he'd missed something. A tiny bit of hope blossomed as he studied the words, hurried letters scrawled on the paper. Letting himself have hope angered him. He let that anger win because hope hurt too much.

Pounding a fist against his desk, Hudson leapt to his feet, knocking his chair down in the process. "Is this some kind of horrible joke, Ava? Why would you do this *now*? After all these years!"

His bellow filled the room, reverberating between them for a full sixty seconds as Ava remained seated, picking at a thread in the fabric of her purse. "You tell me, Hudson. Why *would* I do something like that?" She stood up and paced the floor in front of his desk. "I mean, it makes perfect sense to destroy my home just to irritate you, don't you think?" She stopped walking and faced him with her hands on her hips.

His face burned with agitation, and that vein at the side of his neck had to be visibly throbbing. "Honestly, Ava, I have no idea." Hudson moved out from behind the desk, crossing his arms over his chest as he came around to lean on its edge right in front of Ava. He glared at her.

She was so close, they almost touched. His heart skipped a little beat as memories of a long-ago time tried to flood his mind. Pushing them aside, Hudson steeled himself with his anger.

Not surprisingly, she met his glare with one of her own. "I guess I probably dropped that baby off at the church, too, just so I'd have a reason to torture you. On this day of all days. She was my *best friend*, Hudson. I miss her too! Don't you get it? You're not the only one who lost Quinn that day!"

He'd always expected Ava to move on, the memory of that day and the date on the calendar fading with each passing year. Seeing her that morning and now, the anguish in her eyes behind the hard stare she leveled on him, told him she still felt Quinn's death deeply. As much or maybe even a little more than he did.

"You know what? This was a total waste of time. I'm sorry I bothered you, Hudson. I'll go make my report at the front desk." Grabbing the sheet of paper, she then stepped around him and headed to the door.

The idiocy of his behavior knocked the wind out of him. If anyone else had shown up in his office, he would have had a completely different reaction.

In two long strides, he reached Ava, stepping between her and the door. "Wait. I'm sorry." He ran his fingers through his hair and took a deep breath. "The note, it caught me off guard. RoD BFF was a Quinn thing."

Hudson reached for the paper, but she side-stepped his grasp.

"I know." Ava moved away from him. "I need this to file my police report."

"No you don't. It's evidence, first of all, and second, I'll take your report."

She shook her head. "I really shouldn't have come

to you. I knew it would be a shock. Maybe it was too much, hitting you with this." Her shoulders relaxed some, and she let out a long breath. "I have to have faith that it could mean Quinn is alive. Pastor always says God works in mysterious ways."

He crossed his arms over his chest. "Why did God take ten years to work, then? Personally, I think this note is just a cruel joke."

"This is not a joke, Hudson. Do you think there's absolutely no chance at all that this could be from Quinn? That your sister is alive and needs our help?"

"I don't know. I hope there is, but... I don't know. It's not concrete proof of anything. It's just six stupid letters."

Ava frowned. "How about the boulder in my house? Is that concrete enough for you?"

Hudson shut his laptop and stowed it in a bag. "I'm not sure it's related. I don't know how it could be. It's more likely connected to the guy following you this morning."

"What if all three are related?" she asked.

He sighed. "Let's just go have a look. I was about to head out for the night anyway."

She rested her hands on her hips with a light glare. "I showed you a picture. You don't need to go to my house."

"Come on, Ava. I already know where you live. Sunrise is a really small town." He reached for her hand out of some old, forgotten habit and jerked his arm back when he realized what he'd done.

She stared at him with so many questions in her eyes and quite a few shadows as well. Were those shadows of memories, like the ones he carried tucked into a corner of his heart he no longer acknowledged?

"I'm sorry." He ran his fingers through his hair again. "I don't know why I did that."

She shrugged. "Don't worry about it. Some habits die hard, I guess."

Ava pulled the door open and walked out, leaving him standing there trying to compose himself. This day had not turned out to be anything like he'd expected. At the moment, he had no idea if that was a good thing or a bad one.

THREE

Frustrated by the conversation they'd just had, Ava didn't know how to interact with Hudson right then. She just knew she needed a little space before they were in her house together.

For a second, she thought maybe he believed her, and they would work together to find Quinn, whom Ava was now 100 percent certain wasn't dead. She felt it in her gut. When he'd said he wanted to see the rock himself, she wasn't sure if he was taking it seriously or if he just wanted to find a way to discredit her. He didn't believe Quinn could still be alive. He didn't *want* to believe it. That would call into question everything he'd accepted as true. Well, she *did* believe it was possible, and obviously going to Hudson Pierce for help had been a huge mistake. She'd show him the rock, then show him the door right back out of her life again. After that, she'd find Quinn herself.

Ava had made it half a block when Hudson called out to her. "Ava! It's not safe. Come back! I'll drive us there."

Ignoring him, she kept walking. If he knew where she lived, he could find his own way. Being locked in the cab of a truck with Hudson, even for a few minutes, held absolutely no appeal for her at the moment.

An engine hummed beside her, but she refused to look over.

"Ava. Get in the truck." His annoyance was clearly conveyed through his tone of voice, making her more determined to *not* go with him.

"I like to walk. Thanks anyway."

Without making eye contact, she followed the same route home she'd originally taken to the police station, hoping he'd just give up and move on. Instead, the truck continued to roll slowly alongside her, aggravating her even more.

When he called out to her again, Ava finally stopped moving and glared up at him.

"Stop using your cop voice on me," she demanded, her hands on her hips and anger tightening her chest. "I'm not some perp you're trying to arrest."

"A perp I'm trying to arrest? You've been watching too many cop dramas on television."

His laughter angered her even more. She turned and began walking again. "Shut up and go away, Hudson. I'm sorry I even brought you into this."

"Aw, come on, Ava. Get in the truck. There's debris everywhere. I'd feel a whole lot better if you'd let me drive you. Please."

She didn't even stop to look over at him. "I'm not sure why you'd care now. After all this time."

"That's not fair, Ava. Quinn was the only family I had left, and she drowned while I... and you... and—" He swallowed so hard, she actually heard the gulp in his throat.

"We weren't doing anything wrong. You've been so convinced she died that you've spent a decade holding a grudge and carrying the weight of guilt everywhere. I *knew* there was no way Quinn could drown out there, but you'd never listen to me. You were ready to assume the worst on day one. Now that I might have proof she's alive, you're suddenly concerned for my safety?"

She knew she'd barely made sense, but nothing about any of it made sense at the moment.

Hudson turned off the truck and jumped down onto the sidewalk. Moving so he stood right in front of her, close enough that she could smell the familiar scent that had always been just his, he stared down at her. "It's not proof. All it does is raise a mess of questions I have no answers for. And, just for the record, I have never stopped being concerned. Nor have I blamed you for Quinn's death."

"Liar, liar, pants on fire." As soon as the childish words left her mouth, horror replaced her anger. Hudson always made her say something dumb. Embarrassed, she brushed past him and jogged away. Her face burned with annoyance at how quickly he could still get to her. Just like when they were kids.

Hudson must have given up and gotten back into his vehicle. He passed her a few seconds later. By the time she reached the sidewalk in front of her house where he was waiting, the heat in her face had partially subsided but not her aggravation with how he flustered her, *still*. He looked too much like the old Hudson, her first schoolgirl crush, her first kiss, and, if she were being completely honest, her first real love.

With his thumbs hooked in the back pockets of his jeans, he leaned against his truck, studying the damage to her front window. He let out a low whistle. "They took out the entire window."

She stopped about five feet away from him. "Why do you say 'they'?"

He pointed at some impressions in the wet lawn. "I can't make out any details, but these imprints are definitely two different sizes."

Ava peered at the ground. "Yeah, okay. I can see it. I suppose it would take more than one person to throw that boulder into my house."

Hudson scanned the rest of the area. "Did you hear or see anything out here before it happened?"

"Um, how about a major storm? The only thing louder than that was glass shattering all over my house."

He gestured at her tree-covered car. "That must have made quite a racket."

She shrugged. "It probably did. Hard to hear anything while hiding in my bathtub, though."

Hudson chuckled. "You're still afraid of thunder and lightning?"

"I am not!" Ava sighed. He had a memory like an elephant. "I just wanted to be prepared for the tornado."

"Oh, the tornado? Did you see a funnel?" He pulled out his phone. "I need to report that."

"Hudson."

He punched in several numbers. "Get me the guy at NOAA. Thanks."

"Hudson!" She grabbed for his arm. "Hang up the call."

"Why?" He looked at her, his expression full of mirth again.

Ava looked away, feeling the heat return to her face. "There was no funnel cloud. I just wanted to be ready. You know, just in case."

For a split second, as his smile almost reached his eyes, Ava thought she saw the old Hudson Pierce, awkward teenager with a mouth full of braces, trying to kiss her and not cut her lip with his inexperienced attempts.

He showed her the screen on his phone. "I know there was no tornado. I didn't call anyone."

"You're making fun of me."

He shook his head. "No. Well, maybe, just a little. Sorry."

His sheepish look brought back a waterfall of memories—more things she'd worked hard to tuck away forever—and now she just felt confused and annoyed.

Ava walked up the stairs to the little front porch and unlocked the door. Hudson still stood in the yard, taking pictures of the outside of her house.

"Are you coming?" she called back over her shoulder as she entered the cottage. Dropping her purse onto a table in the hall, she then flicked a switch, expecting the power to still be out. She wasn't disappointed. Ava waded through the water and debris littering her living room floor toward the kitchen.

Hudson let out another low whistle. She assumed he'd seen the mess. After grabbing two bottles of water from the refrigerator and closing the door quickly to conserve as much cold air inside as possible, she returned to what was left of her main living area.

"Water?" she asked, holding one of the bottles out toward him.

"Thanks." He accepted the bottle, his fingers brushing hers lightly as he took it.

Long-forgotten but definitely familiar sparks traveled through her at the accidental touch. Oh, this was so not a good thing.

Hudson pointed at the rock sitting on her wood floor. "That's quite a message."

"I don't get it. 'We know' seems sort of lame." She took a sip of her water and set it on the coffee table.

"I meant the giant boulder sitting in the middle of the room. But yeah, that message isn't very specific. Are you in any kind of trouble? Made any enemies lately?" He moved closer to the rock and snapped a few pictures of it, including a close-up of the painted-on words.

"Until a few hours ago, my life was uncomplicated and peaceful." Not to mention a little bit lonely, but she'd be keeping that part to herself. "It has to be related to the note that came with Eli."

Hudson shook his head. "I just don't see how. The message has nothing to do with a baby or Quinn not actually drowning."

"It has to be related. I mean, first I'm being followed by some creeper, then the baby shows up with a note specifically addressed to me, and then someone destroys my house an hour later."

He walked over and looked out the window. "It just doesn't add up. Why didn't they come in here after you if they just wanted to find the infant? Why throw a rock with a weird message? 'We know.' What do they know?"

"I wish I understood any of this." She walked over to the one chair in the room that didn't appear to be soaked through. Sitting down, she leaned her elbows on her thighs and rested her chin in her hands. "You still don't think Quinn is alive, do you?"

Hudson exhaled. "It would take a miracle, and

quite honestly, I don't believe in miracles. The big guy and I don't have that sort of relationship. In fact, it's quite the opposite. He prefers to take things away from me rather than give them."

"I don't get it. You used to be the one dragging Quinn and me to Sunday school and making us go to all the youth group meet-ups. When did you lose your faith, Hudson?"

She looked so forlorn, sitting there the way a child might after being told her birthday party was canceled. The heart in his chest that had hardened toward Ava Taft years ago—or at least he'd told himself it had—sped up just a little bit as the thought of taking her in his arms to console her briefly passed through his mind.

Steeling himself against any sort of emotion, he turned on the cop version of Hudson Pierce. The part he didn't always like but knew had to make an appearance if he was going to get out of there emotionally intact. This whole day just had to end.

"There is no concrete evidence that the baby or the note came from my sister. For all I know, you could have created this whole scenario to get back at me."

She jumped out of the chair, her green eyes blazing with anger. "Get *back* at you? Are you insane?"

He leaned against a wall, his arms folded across his chest. Working hard at maintaining a disinterested expression, he hoped his voice didn't give away the emotions he tried to ignore. "What should I think, then? Next thing you'll be telling me is that my parents have been on vacation since I was in high school."

She paced the room. "I mean, I guess it makes perfect sense. I could have stolen a baby at the supermarket, written the note, and then magically made the baby appear in the foyer of the church while I was very clearly sitting in the front of the sanctuary, listening to the sermon. What's a hundred or so witnesses?" Ava stopped pacing and looked through the hole where the window used to be. "I think you're absolutely correct, Detective Pierce. It all points to me."

The more she talked, the more ridiculous he realized he'd sounded. Letting Ava know that was out of the question, though. If he admitted to her that he knew it wasn't her, then he'd have to admit to himself that it could actually have been his dead sister.

Presumed dead sister.

The documentation provided to him by the court had said "presumed dead." No body—no remains at all—were ever found. They'd all assumed she'd been pulled out to sea by the strong rip currents that day. Her body swallowed up by the ocean and all its depths.

No. There was no way. If Quinn had been alive all these years, he would have known. A detective would have known. Gut instinct and all that stuff they talked about. A *brother* would have known.

"Honestly, Ava. I have no idea what to think. All I know is it's a little too convenient that all this has happened on the anniversary of Quinn's death. Almost like someone had planned it all."

"Yes!" She threw her hands up in the air, exasperation replacing the anger in her expression. "That's what I'm trying to get you to understand. And it all points to the one person who it shouldn't logically point to."

Ava looked very pleased with her assessment of the entire situation. Even as a kid, when they were all playing in the sand together at the beach, she would get that look as they built castles and dug moats.

His phone rang in his back pocket. Hudson pulled it out and hit Answer on the screen. "Pierce."

"Detective Pierce, this is Janet James with Child Protective Services. I just wanted to let you know that we have found a placement for the boy until you can locate his mother."

He sighed. "That could take some time. I'm glad you found a family to take him in."

There was the sound of some papers being shuffled on Janet's end of the call before she spoke again. "The boy is very well cared for. The clothing and other items that were with him are well made and probably very expensive. This was no random abandoned child."

Hudson nodded as she spoke, taking in the information she shared. "Thank you for letting me know, Ms. James. If you learn anything else, please give me a call."

"You are very welcome, Detective. I will be in touch."

Ava sat quietly during the exchange. When he ended the call, she asked, "Is Eli okay?"

He returned his phone to his pocket. "The baby is fine. They found a family for him, and he's being well cared for."

She frowned. "I really wish you would have let me

keep him. I am a licensed foster parent, you know. I went through the process as part of my job training. He could be Quinn's baby. You sent your nephew into the system. Are you okay with that?"

He shook his head. "You know I had to call Child Protective Services for an abandoned baby. And given the danger you've been in since he showed up, it's probably safer for him anyway."

She nodded. "I suppose you're right. But I am not at all happy about it. At least that means we can focus on finding Quinn."

He held up a hand. "Hold on there. This is not a 'we' thing. And who said anything about finding Quinn? Quinn has been dead for a long time."

Ava's angry glare caught him a little off guard. "Hudson! You can't just cut me out of the case!"

"First of all, there is no case. At least not the one you want there to be. And second, yes I can. You're an adoption agent, not a detective. Your part of this is over and done with." He walked toward the front door. "I'm going to write this up. I'll send you a copy of the report to your office for insurance purposes."

She followed him. "Please let me help you find Quinn."

Before he opened the door, he turned to look at her. The sadness in her eyes ran deep and was almost hidden behind all the other emotions. Ava missed Quinn as much as he did. If only it hadn't been their fault she disappeared, he might be able to stand to be around her. Right now, though, he had to get some serious distance between them. They could never go back, and the only way he knew how to keep moving forward was to let this part of his past go once and for all.

"There is no open case on Quinn. We won't be looking for her. She's gone, Ava."

"I don't believe it, and I know you don't either!"

"Goodbye, Ava." He gestured to her living room. "Get that window covered, and be careful. You've obviously upset someone."

Without another word, he opened the door and walked out of Ava's house. Hopefully, it was for the last time. He wasn't sure he could handle another encounter.

That tiny little voice in the back of his mind that he worked hard at ignoring whispered to him the one thing he couldn't accept. *It was an accident.*

Accidents had claimed way too much from him. There was no one to blame for an accident, and without blame, he'd never be able to cope. The ocean had taken way too much. It had to be *someone's* fault.

How could Quinn have allowed herself to drown, especially knowing how their parents had died?

Maybe if he hadn't been so busy tasting Ava's cherry lip gloss, he wouldn't have lost the last person in his family.

Maybe he should have gone in the water with his sister rather than beneath the pier with his sister's best friend.

So. Many. Maybes.

FOUR

No electricity meant no air conditioning. Once Hudson left, she'd dug an old tarp out of the shed out back and created a makeshift cover for the gaping hole in her house. Two hours of mopping and wiping things down got rid of the excess standing water. She tossed the storm debris into the trash can and dragged the area rug out to the backyard where she hung it over the rail of the small deck. Without air conditioning, though, her house was far too humid to even begin to dry out the furniture.

The heat and humidity took a toll on her too. Even after a cold shower to clean up after her storm adventures, Ava still couldn't cool down. Grabbing a small bag from her bedroom closet, she tossed a few necessities inside along with a change of clothes and some extra tennis shoes. After packing some sandwich fixings and a few bottles of water in an insulated bag, she headed out the front door. Locking up seemed useless given the ratty blue tarp tacked around her window opening, but there was no sense in inviting more trouble.

Knowing she was taking a huge chance that her office even had power, Ava set out on the two-mile walk to the other side of the town center, rubber rain boots splashing through the standing water all around her. Several of the solar-powered streetlights came on as she walked, but the stoplights sat dark. Branches, some as long as she was tall, littered the street, even blocking one major intersection. Several crews from the power company were out, trying to repair the lines and restore electricity. The entire town seemed eerily quiet, her footsteps and the engines of the work trucks the only sounds she heard.

By the time she made it to the agency's building, the sun had completely set, and her previously dry clothes clung to her. She may as well have not even showered.

It only took a few seconds to punch in the security code to unlock the door and step inside to the glorious feel of ice-cold air wrapping around her overheated body.

"Thank you, God. I'm not sure what I would have done if the power were out here too."

Setting the bag she carried on her desk, Ava walked to the little room where they kept a refrigerator and a microwave. Her stomach let out a loud growl as she unpacked her groceries. She needed to eat soon, but everything she brought felt a little lukewarm, so she wanted it to chill a bit first. In the meantime, there was plenty of research to do.

Back at her desk, she powered up her laptop. She sat in the dark, enjoying the cold air blowing on her from the vent in the ceiling above her and waiting for the search engine to load.

In her time as a placement specialist at the adoption agency, Ava had learned many search tricks to try and locate people who didn't want to be found. As she typed "Quinn Pierce" into the search engine, she held her breath.

Several queries popped up. All of them about her death, her parents' death, and later about a handful of memorials that had been held in her honor. Once she'd combed through all the articles, Ava switched gears and started searching birth records from the last six months. If she could find a baby boy named Elijah born locally, she might have a place to start.

What she discovered was that the name Elijah had been very popular during the last six months. Printing the long list of babies to follow up on later, she closed her laptop and went to make a sandwich.

The tiny break room, which was no bigger than a large closet, connected her office to her boss's office. Jillian and Ava were the only ones who worked for the small church-sponsored agency, and they actually liked each other, so the doors usually sat open, essentially connecting their workspaces.

She passed through the kitchen and into Jillian's office at the front of the building. Oddly, the main entrance was on the back side of the building, but Jillian had a huge window that overlooked the sidewalk and Main Street beyond. As Ava stood there in the shadows, looking out at the dark center of town, she caught sight of two figures moving toward the alley that led to their door.

Had she remembered to reset the alarm when she let herself in?

Ava glanced at the keypad on the wall across the room. It showed a bright green light. The alarm was off. Moving as quietly as she could, she headed to the keypad. Just before she reached her destination, she heard the main door open and voices filtering down the hall. She froze, scanning the room for someplace to hide.

"Boss says we better find out where that brat is," one of the intruders said.

Someone else grunted. "If you ask me, things are a lot better around that place without all the crying and dirty diapers and stuff."

Something heavy tipped over and crashed to the floor.

Ava scooted silently to Jillian's desk and climbed into the little space underneath it. Holding her breath, she waited to see if she'd been heard.

"You go through the file cabinet. See if you can get an address. I'll deal with the computer."

She clapped a hand over her mouth. Her computer! All the searches and the papers she'd printed were still there. If these men were looking for Eli....

"There's nothing here!" the other guy, who sounded much younger than the first, said. Something else crashed when it hit the floor.

"Hey, come here and look at this." Both men were quiet for a good bit before the crashing and banging started up again.

The search of her office seemed to last forever as

she stayed as still as she could. Finally, when the cuckoo clock on Jillian's wall chimed eleven times, the office went completely quiet.

Had they left?

Please let them be gone.

Ava waited another twenty minutes, listening to the tick of the clock in the silence of the office before climbing out from under the desk and peeking out the window. No sign of anyone. The streets were darker and emptier than they had been when she'd arrived, even with the stoplights restored. No one was outside doing anything. Of course, at midnight in a town as small as Sunrise, nothing ever really happened anyway.

Except for random babies showing up at the church, rocks flying through windows, and her office being completely destroyed.

Ava stepped through the tiny kitchen area and into her own office space. The entire place had been ransacked. Her files had been strewn everywhere. The chair to her desk was tipped to the side and blocked her path to the door. Everything was everywhere.

And her laptop was gone! Whoever took it would know what she'd been searching. If they had been there because of Quinn and Eli, she may have just put them both in serious jeopardy.

Scrambling through the mess, she turned on the alarm and locked all the doors. Jillian was out of town for the next two weeks, so no one would need to get in, and she certainly didn't want to go out at the moment. Everything in her screamed, *Call Hudson!* But she resisted. He'd made it perfectly clear that he had no interest in anything having to do with her. Ava was on her own, and the thought of the trouble she might be in scared her more than she wanted to admit.

HUDSON SPENT THE NEXT HOUR AFTER LEAVING Ava's house working on the report she'd need for her insurance company. It worried him that she would be alone in that house all night. He should have boarded the window up for her. Then he got mad at himself for worrying. If only he hadn't been on duty that morning when the church call went out. He'd still be keeping his happy distance from the person responsible for changing his entire life rather than considering dropping by with the report and checking on her.

Once he'd uploaded the photos he'd taken of the rock, her living room, and the window from the outside, Hudson hit Save and printed a copy for his own files as well as a second copy for Ava.

The clock told him it was basically the middle of the night. He would just drive by and leave the envelope in her mailbox. That way she could get that window fixed sooner rather than later.

He could probably send it to her work email address listed on the agency website. A hand-delivered hard copy would be more efficient, though. He grabbed his baseball hat and keys and headed out the door.

The short drive took no time at all. As he pulled his truck to a stop in front of Ava's tiny cottage for the second time that night, he sucked in a breath.

The front door was wide open, and the beat-up old tarp only half covered the window hole. The darkness of all the houses on the block told him the power hadn't yet been reconnected from the storm.

Checking the gun on his hip more out of habit than anything, Hudson then jumped from the truck and silently moved through the night and onto the small porch.

Only silence greeted him. Silence and a huge mess. Someone had torn through the house, turning over furniture and dumping out drawers as they ransacked the place. His pulse kicked up a notch with worry. Walking quietly, he searched each room for a possible burglar still on-site.

A floorboard creaked. He froze. No other sounds came, so he moved silently again. Maybe it was just the old house creaking. Old houses did that sometimes.

As he neared one of the bedrooms, he heard the sound of an engine roaring to life and tires spinning against the pavement.

Someone *had been* in the house.

Please let Ava be okay.

Just because he was angry at her didn't mean he wanted anything bad to happen to her. Through the tiny kitchen, he could see that the back door was wide open. When he finally got to it, he'd cleared the entire house and found no sign of the intruder. Or Ava.

He holstered his weapon. Had the rock throwers returned and grabbed her this time?

The knot in his gut belied his worry for the woman he had basically told to stay out of his life just a couple hours ago. The cop part of him wouldn't sleep tonight if he didn't know Ava was safe. The broken-man part of him tried to convince the other part he didn't care.

He locked the back door with the dead bolt, then returned to the living room. He couldn't do much with the shredded edges of the tarp, but he could lock the front door and make it a little harder for someone to get back inside.

Once he'd secured the house, Hudson returned to his truck and tried to decide if Ava was missing or just at a different location.

Her office was close by. If he were in her position with no air conditioner on a hot and humid summer night, he'd go see if the office could offer relief. He told himself he was just doing his job by going to check on her.

Hudson slowly cruised the block a couple times, checking yards as he drove, just to make sure there were no lurkers possibly waiting for Ava. Finally, he turned the truck toward the small downtown area and her office.

Five minutes later, he spotted lights on in the storefront office the adoption agency rented. A silhouette that looked very similar to Ava's shone through the curtains.

"Thank goodness." He climbed out of his truck.

Following the sign that pointed down a narrow

alleyway to the door of the building, he stopped when he reached the entrance. Hudson knocked hard enough for Ava to hear him in the front. When she didn't answer, he banged on it a little more forcefully. He could hear movement inside and then a small crash of something breaking.

Knocking loudly one more time, he debated kicking in the door. She could be in trouble.

As he'd just about made up his mind to do so, he heard a familiar voice. Ava.

"Don't come in here! I have a gun, and I'll use it!"

He knew better. Ava hated guns. At least she had ten years ago, and he couldn't imagine that having changed.

"Ava! Open the door!" he called through the glass. "It's me, Hudson."

A few beeps told him the alarm system had been disabled. One of the locks turned, and Ava pulled the door open slowly.

She peeked through the narrow gap. She held something in her hand, poised to hit him on the head with it. "It's two in the morning. What are you doing here, Hudson? And, actually, how did you even find me?"

"I went by your house, and you weren't there." A

noise down the alley caught his attention. "Can you let me in, please?"

She frowned. "Why? I got the impression earlier that you were still done with me, like you were after Quinn disappeared."

There went that noise again. He scanned the area once more, but it was just too dark to see anything. "Please let me in. I have something for you."

"Unless it's a huge apology, I'm not interested." She started to close the door, but he shoved his boot between the jamb and the door, blocking the move.

"They were at your house again. The whole place was torn apart." Something rubbed against his ankles. "What the heck is that?" He kicked at it, making contact. The creature let out a loud screech and a hiss.

Ava lowered her hand with the object in it. "You hurt Fred."

"Fred?"

"Our resident stray alley cat. He's very affectionate and just wanted you to pet him." She pulled the door open. "So, someone trashed my house. What do you think they were looking for? And why were you at my house?"

Hudson stepped forward, placing himself more

inside than out. "Let's sit down and try to figure it out."

Ava nodded and motioned him in. She closed and triple-checked the locks on the door, then reset the alarm.

"What happened here?" He looked around the trashed office.

She shrugged. "I guess the same thing that happened at my house. Only I was here for this one."

"You were here? Did they see you?" He tried to ignore the panic rising into his throat at the thought of Ava being found by the men who were obviously looking for something they thought she had.

She shrugged. "Obviously not, Detective, or I suspect we wouldn't be having this conversation. I hid under the desk in Jillian's office. Whatever they wanted must have been in mine, and they never went anywhere else except there." She sighed. "They took my laptop, though."

"What have you gone and gotten yourself into?" Hudson walked down the hall and into her office. He took up residence in the chair opposite her desk as if he'd been doing that his whole life.

"Nothing! I haven't done anything except find homes for babies who don't have anyone." She frowned. "Like I said, they took my laptop, though, so they think I know something about *something*."

He leaned back and crossed one leg over the other. "I'm going to hazard a guess that this has something to do with the baby who showed up at the church this morning. If they took your laptop, then they must think his location is on it."

"One of them said their boss told them to find 'the brat.'"

Hudson nodded. "Then it is about the baby."

"So, why tear up my house?" She looked concerned but not scared.

He shrugged. "I'm guessing they thought you took it home for the weekend."

Ava sighed heavily as she motioned to the mess. "I don't even want to take myself home now. I'll stay here for a few days. We only found Eli twelve hours ago. They must be desperate to get to him, for whatever reason."

He leaned forward and looked her in the eye. "There's no logical explanation for any of this other than wanting the baby back. I'm not sure what to make of anything that happened today. My gut tells me this is somehow related to it being the anniversary of Quinn's death. I just don't know how. Or why.

I'm still trying to figure out why anyone would abandon a baby and then work so hard to get it back."

She sat down at her desk and leaned forward, resting her folded arms on the surface. "I know it doesn't make sense. What have I done to attract this sort of... attention from men like that? Unless it has something to do with Quinn."

Hudson didn't even want to think about his sister being a part of this. If he did, he'd have to consider the fact that maybe he'd been wrong about her disappearance. That wasn't something he was prepared to do. He knew how investigations worked, and if the police determined there was no way she could still be alive, he had to accept that, or what sort of cop, and brother, was he?

"I don't think it has anything to do with Quinn. She's been gone a long time. I do think someone wants us to *think* it's about her, though."

She narrowed her eyes at him, forming a tiny crease just above the bridge of her nose. He didn't remember those lines being there before. Of course, ten years had passed, and a lot had changed. He expected her to say something about how stubborn he was or how wrong he'd been, but instead she just leaned back in her chair and sighed again, like she'd changed her mind about whatever she'd been about to say.

"You still haven't told me why you were at my house again. Or, for that matter, why you're even here."

He pulled the envelope out of his back jeans pocket. "I brought you the police report on the rock for your insurance company." He handed it over to her.

Ava narrowed her eyes, suspicion clouding her expression. "You could have emailed it to me."

Hudson shrugged. Yeah, he could have. He probably should have, because now he felt even more deeply involved in something he didn't understand with the one person he had wanted to avoid for, well, the rest of his life.

Instead of responding to her last comment, he shrugged again. "Do you know how lucky you are that they didn't find you under that desk?"

Ava frowned at his question. "Yeah, I guess so."

He leaned in, closing the distance between them some so she would have to look him directly in the eyes. "They would have hurt you. Kidnapped you, maybe. Killed you eventually."

"We don't even know who *they* are or what they

wanted." She gave a little wave of her hand. "I'm fine. That's all that matters."

Her blasé attitude frustrated him. "You're fine because they didn't know you were here. And that's nothing short of a small miracle."

She stood up and started straightening the mess in her office. "I'm really surprised you care. A few hours ago, you couldn't push me back out of your life fast enough."

Hudson also stood up and began gathering files from the floor. "I know. This is hard, Ava. I spent the last ten years dealing with my sister's death and blaming myself. Blaming us."

"You have to let it go. Move on with your life." She stopped and looked over at him. "We were kids, Hudson. How could any of it be our fault?"

"You mean you never blamed yourself?"

The light bulb in the lamp beside her head exploded.

"Get down!" Hudson shoved Ava to the floor as he pulled his gun from the holster on his hip. He ran to the window and yanked open the curtains to find a bullet hole in the glass and a dark-colored SUV speeding off down the street.

Turning back, he squatted down by her. "They're gone. Are you okay?"

"Yeah, I'm good." She lifted her head to look at him. Blood trailed down the right side of her face.

Hudson sucked in a breath. A knot formed in his stomach as reality kicked him hard in the gut. She could have died right there in front of him, and he'd been a complete and total ass for an entire decade.

"No you're not." He reached up and pushed her hair back behind her ear, away from the blood. "You're bleeding."

She touched the spot, studying the red liquid with her fingers. "I didn't feel anything. It must be from the light bulb breaking. I have a first aid kit in the bathroom. I'll go clean up."

He offered her a hand to help her stand up, but she shrugged it away, using the desk to support herself. "See? I'm fine."

She stumbled a little as all the color washed out of her face.

Hudson caught her as her knees buckled. "Don't worry, I've got you."

Ava reached up and pressed her palm to his cheek. "Liar, liar, pants on fire."

Her eyes closed as her body went limp.

FIVE

Sunlight saturated the room. Ava covered her eyes with an arm. "Ugh. Why is it so bright in here?"

Someone chuckled. "It's called sunlight."

Hudson.

She sat up straight, ignoring the room spinning around her. Keeping her eyes narrowed against the brightness, she scowled at him. "What are you doing here?"

He sat in a chair across the room, drinking something from an insulated tumbler. "Well, considering I live here, it does make perfect sense."

"You don't live in my office."

He chuckled. "No. But I do live in my house. Where you currently are."

Things didn't add up. Last thing she remembered, she and Hudson were having a very difficult discussion. Now she was sitting in his—she glanced around the space—living room. "Why am I at your house? I was perfectly happy at my office."

"You don't remember?" He looked worried. "Someone fired a shot through the window. It hit the lamp."

She reached up and touched her temple, feeling a bandage. "The light bulb exploded and cut my head. I do remember now. But how did we get here?"

He took a sip of his drink. She caught a light whiff of coffee that made her mouth water. "I think the adrenaline crash got to you. The injury is just a scratch. I cleaned the area and bandaged it. I couldn't get all the blood or glass in your hair, but the wound is good for now. You'd been on a roller coaster of adrenaline yesterday, and your system probably overloaded."

"But why are we *here*?" The intimacy of sitting in Hudson's home, his private space, after all that had happened made her extremely uncomfortable.

He set his cup down and leaned back, resting his hands on his thighs. "I figured you'd be safer here than at your place or your office, since they've both been breached."

"Breached. What an interesting choice of words." Ava sighed. "I just wish I understood everything that's going on. Why is anyone trying to breach me?"

Hudson raised an eyebrow at her own choice of words but didn't comment.

She shifted so she sat leaning against the back cushion. "You think that maybe Quinn knew where we would be yesterday, and she planned it?"

"Why are you so convinced that Quinn had anything to do with this?" He smacked a hand down on the arm of the chair. "Why haven't you ever accepted that she is dead?" Hudson jumped to his feet and paced the room.

Ava knew it had been absolutely infuriating to him that she had insisted for so long that his sister was out there somewhere. She just couldn't believe he still felt so strongly about it.

"Quinn drowned, Ava! Ten years ago. You have to move on!"

"*I* have to move on?" Her voice rose a little, which annoyed her. "What about you?"

Hudson stopped to stare at her. Maybe glare was the more appropriate description. If looks could shoot daggers.... "She was my sister. The only family I had left. If I thought for a second that she might have survived, I would have scoured the ocean myself."

He walked over to stare out the window. His expression changed to one she couldn't read. "Quinn was so smart. And always had a plan. She could swim like a pro. How did she let herself drown?"

He sounded so incredibly sad. Heartbroken, even after so many years.

Ava sighed. "Neither of us knows what actually happened out there. And we can't go back to change it." Rehashing the same thing over and over and opening wounds that had already healed gave her a headache. She stood up slowly, making sure everything stayed steady. "Can you point me to the bathroom and then maybe the coffeepot?"

Turning from the window, he motioned toward the back of the house. "Bathroom is halfway down the hall, and the kitchen is at the end. This is a small place, so I'm sure you'll find it."

Leaving him where he stood staring out the window, Ava found the bathroom. Her reflection caught her off guard. Hudson had bandaged her cut, but there were still several tiny little sparkles in her hair, presumably from the destroyed light bulb. Streaks of dried blood ran along her hairline. Splashing a little cold water on her face, she wiped away the stains and patted her skin dry with a towel she found on the counter.

A little less horrified at her reflection, Ava left the bathroom, giving herself a pep talk as she walked. "Time for coffee. Then we figure out what's really going on around here." It only took a minute to find herself a mug and pour a cup of coffee. She could hear Hudson talking in the living room. She guessed someone must have called him while she was in the bathroom. Gripping the mug with both hands, she enjoyed the warmth it gave off. The view outside the kitchen window intrigued her. Lush greenery, brilliant colors over a broad array of tropical-looking flowers and at least a dozen birdhouses, feeders, and hummingbird feeders dotting the landscape. A slate pathway wound through the space, ending at a small pond with a fountain in the center. On the bank of the pond, a large orange cat lay in the shade of low-hanging crepe myrtle branches.

"I never would have guessed this side of you, Hudson." After taking another sip from the mug and finally beginning to feel human, she turned to head back to the living room and found Hudson standing in the doorway.

Ava gasped, her face filling with heat for being caught talking to herself. She grinned through her embarrassment. "You're like a ninja. I never heard you coming."

He didn't even crack a smile as he walked over and stood beside her, his expression distant as he looked out the window. "I've spent a lot of time out there over the years. It's been my distraction. A cure for some of the loneliness, I guess."

"I'm so sorry you've had to deal with that alone all these years." She gave him a pointed look. "We could have dealt with it together, but you cut me out of your life."

Shaking his head, Hudson set his phone on the little breakfast table next to his own coffee cup. "It was our fault, Ava. We should have stayed with her. The rip currents were rough that day. We let her go in the water alone so we could—" His words were emotionless, his expression blank. "How could I have gone on with my life when hers was cut way too short? Knowing I might have been able to do something about it made it that much worse."

Ava set her mug down and turned to look at Hudson. He made no move to stop staring out the window, but she took a deep breath and continued with what she wanted to say. "If, and now I think that's a *big* if, Quinn drowned, then it was an accident. We were kids, Hudson. How could we have saved her if a rip current got her? Quinn grew up on the ocean. She knew what to do. If she couldn't get out of it, what were we supposed to do?"

She picked up her cup and took another sip of the now lukewarm liquid. "I don't think she died out there, though. I never could quite accept it, and the appearance of Eli proves it."

Hudson slammed his palms down on the quartz countertop. "It doesn't prove anything!"

Ava watched as he stormed out of the house, letting the heavy door to the backyard slam shut behind him. Through the window she could see him crossing the yard to the little pond, where he dropped down onto a stone bench. He leaned down and picked up a handful of the little white rocks that surrounded the chair and one by one skipped them across the pond. The big orange cat lifted its head and eyed him lazily before returning to its nap.

As she debated whether or not she should go talk to him, his cell phone that he'd left on the breakfast table rang. Glancing at the screen, she saw the letters CPS. Child Protective Services. Had something happened to little Eli?

Grabbing the phone, she ran out back to where Hudson sat. He looked over as she approached. Ava handed it to him. "This might be about the baby."

He nodded as he took the cell phone and

answered the call, turning on the speaker function. "Detective Pierce."

"Hello, Detective. This is Janet James."

"Hi, Ms. James. How are you this morning?"

"I'm afraid I have some unsettling news. The foster parents who took in Elijah are unable to keep him. They've had a family emergency and have to go out of town on an extended trip. We have nowhere else to place him at the moment, so he'll be staying in a group facility until we locate a suitable placement."

"That's terrible!" Ava exclaimed, clapping a hand to her mouth after a look from Hudson.

"What was that, Detective?" Ms. James asked.

He held a finger to lips, telling her not to say any more. "Nothing, ma'am. Sorry about that."

Ava mouthed, "Where?"

Hudson nodded. "Can you tell me which facility he's at? I might like to check in on the little guy from time to time."

Janet exhaled loudly. "Telling you that is highly unusual per policy, Detective Pierce. But, given the unusual circumstances, I'll text you the address. That baby needs someone to care about him."

"Thank you, Ms. James. I really appreciate it. A little guy like that, it's just such a shame."

Ava waited as Hudson said goodbye and disconnected the call before she spoke again. "Well? Can we go see him?"

He held up a hand as he cracked a little smile. "Hold on, now. She said she'd text me the address, but I can't just march in there with you and demand to see him."

"But you said... and she said...." She frowned, unable to get the words out.

"Ava, I'm a police officer. The detective who responded when the baby was found. They'll let me in. You're technically just a stranger, and there are rules about that stuff, especially with kids."

"Tell them I'm your partner." She walked to the edge of the little pond and looked down. Brightly colored koi swam in the clear water. Her reflection wavered like her emotions—all over the place. She exhaled slowly, her shoulders slumping. "Never mind, I know you can't do that."

AVA LOOKED SO FORLORN THAT IT CHIPPED away a little at the ice that had long ago formed around his heart. He'd been so lost in his own grief that he'd never once considered she might be hurting just as much. Over the last twenty-four hours, he'd begun to get a better understanding of that.

She jumped a little when he rested a hand on her shoulder. "I'll see what I can figure out. Maybe I can sneak you in there for a minute or two. Would that help?"

"I just need to know he's okay." Swiping away some tears, Ava sniffed. "I've missed Quinn so much, and now we might have an actual living connection to her, and we can't see him or touch him. It's just so unfair."

Her steadfast belief that Eli was his dead sister's baby aggravated him to no end. Why couldn't she let it go? "It's not Quinn's baby. She's dead, Ava. You have to accept that."

Hudson bristled at the coldness of his own voice. The hurt on her face almost made him regret his words. The truth often really hurt, though, and as much as he wanted to believe Quinn was out there somewhere, alive, the odds were stacked against it— note or no note. Ava needed to accept the truth and deal with the hurt.

His phone made a sound. "Looks like I've got that address. Hmmm... it doesn't seem to be far from here." An idea formed. "Do you want to go look in on him now?"

Her entire face lit up. "Do you mean it?"

"I have an idea, but I'll need you to play along."

Ava nodded. "Of course. Just tell me what I need to do."

Standing up, Hudson headed back toward the house. "Come on. We'll talk on the way. I just need to grab my keys and badge, and then we'll head out."

"I need to wash up a little better. I'll meet you out front after a quick stop at the powder room."

"Okay." He headed to the kitchen, leaving Ava at the hall bathroom. He waited by the front door until she came out much cleaner than she was when she went in.

She shook her hair a little when they stepped outside, lifting it from her shoulders and letting it drop again. "You may have little bits of glass in your sink. I tried to get as much out of my hair as possible without a shower."

"It's okay. When we get back, I'll grab you some clean clothes, and you can take a shower or a bath, whichever you prefer."

"You want me to come back here?" She definitely sounded surprised.

"I don't think you'll be safe at home or your office. Not until we know who's behind all the break-ins. And why."

"Okay." Her tone was noncommittal. He had a feeling she wouldn't come back to his place willingly, but he'd deal with that when it happened. She didn't say anything else as Hudson pulled open the passenger door of his truck for her.

Once they were both settled in the cab of his truck, he headed toward Eli's group home.

Ava fidgeted in her seat.

"You okay?" he asked.

She nodded, tapping her fingers on the door handle. "Just some nervous energy."

Turning the wheel, he took the next left turn. "So, I'm going to tell the manager that I need you to see Eli as part of my investigation. If she questions me, I'm going to hint that there is something going on with illegal adoptions, and you're helping me look into it because you're an expert. I'll let her believe that maybe Eli was saved from some sort of baby trafficking ring."

She turned to look at him. "Baby trafficking? Illegal adoptions? My firm is all above board!"

Hudson chuckled. Her fast-to-ignite temper hadn't changed one bit. "I *know* that, Ava. It's just a cover story—although it's not as unrealistic as you might think. Whoever left Eli very well could have been saving him from something awful."

They passed under a working streetlight. He caught the frown that marred her pretty features in the brief illumination. He'd always hated to see her upset. That was another thing that apparently hadn't changed.

After he took another turn, his GPS informed him the destination was up ahead. Once he found the old Victorian home that had been repurposed, he pulled in, parked, and shut off the truck.

"I don't want them to think my agency is dirty, Hudson. Adoption placement is hard enough. Getting birth mothers to trust us is really difficult."

Without thinking, he reached over and took her hand in his. That same spark from all those years ago fired up between them where they touched—though if Ava felt it, too, she didn't let on. "Trust me, Ava. Please."

Letting go almost as quickly as he'd touched her, Hudson opened the truck door and climbed out. Touching Ava had ignited so many feelings, he actually felt shaky. Considering the hell he'd put her through after Quinn's disappearance, he had no right to ask her to trust him, and he knew it. He took a deep, steadying breath. "Come on. Let's go see the baby. I promise everything will be fine."

Ava didn't reply as she exited the truck. Her face,

especially her eyes, said all the thoughts she wasn't expressing. It hurt his heart to see her so emotionally vulnerable.

Taking her to see Elijah broke so many policies, it would take a week to write the report. His head told him Quinn was dead. But his heart kept saying, *What if?* What if Ava's gut instinct had been right all these years? If the infant had some kind of connection to his sister *and* was "the brat" Ava's pursuers mentioned, could he even begin to hope that his sister was actually alive?

She had always been so certain that her best friend was still out there somewhere. If he let on now that he had even entertained the thought of Quinn being alive, Ava's heart would break all over again when they proved Eli had no connection to his sister.

Hudson sighed and kicked at a stone in the parking lot. If only he'd just taken two weeks off and gone camping or something, then he wouldn't be caught up in any of this. His simple, sad life would have continued on without all these uncomfortable emotions that had stirred since seeing Ava being followed to the cemetery.

Leading the way up a long sidewalk, he kept an eye on their surroundings. Something felt off to his detective's instincts. He just couldn't put a finger on what.

The front door to the home opened as they climbed the wide brick steps. A gray-haired woman in jeans and a pink scrub top looked at them curiously. "What can I do for you two?"

Hudson showed her his badge. "I'm Detective Pierce. Janet James should have told you that I needed access to the boy brought in this morning."

The woman turned her attention to Ava. "Who's she?"

"Ava. She's part of the investigation."

Ava gave a little wave. "Thank you for seeing us on such short notice."

She waved them both up the steps. "Come on inside. It's humid enough to melt a woman right where she stands."

Hudson followed her with Ava close behind him. The woman led them to a large living area filled with couches, chairs, and tables. A single television sat in one corner with the weather broadcasting softly from it.

It shocked him how easily she'd believed his little lie about Ava being part of the investigation. The entire backstory he'd created went unshared.

"If you wait here, Sandy will bring the boy out to

you." She gave them a disapproving look. "He's probably asleep, you know."

Hudson nodded. "I know, and I'm sorry. I wouldn't have asked if it weren't vital to our investigation. I need a few pictures of him and any identifying marks he might have to start the identification process."

That's what had felt so off to him: how quiet everything was. For a house full of children, he'd expected a little chaos. The fact that it was nap time made sense. He relaxed just a little.

"I'm not sure I understand what's so vital about a child abandoned in a church. I mean, yeah, I get that you want to find the mother, but I'm sure that could be done without waking him up?"

There was no mistaking her annoyance, so Hudson put on his best smile and dialed up the charm. "I am so sorry to have disturbed you, and I really hate to wake little Elijah, but his appearance may be connected to another case that's of very high priority. A missing person in extreme danger."

She put her hands on her hips. "Well, I'm not sure what an infant can tell you, but what's done is done." With a little huff she left the room. He heard voices in the hall as Ava tapped her foot incessantly.

Hudson reached over to place a hand on her arm. "Relax, Ava. Please."

She grunted and stepped out of his reach, but the tapping stopped.

A young woman with long, dark braids and a bright smile entered the room, cooing to the baby she carried. She appeared to be much less bothered by their intrusion than her superior.

"Are you here for this little heartbreaker?" she asked Hudson and Ava in a thick Southern drawl. "I sure do hope you can find him a home soon. He is just the sweetest little thing ever, bless his precious soul." Walking past Hudson, she handed Eli to Ava. "Tell me if he doesn't just steal your heart."

Ava's features relaxed instantly as she accepted the bundle of baby and blanket. "Hello, Eli. How are you?"

"See? I told you. I think he'll be very happy with you." The young woman obviously assumed they were there to foster Eli. Ava seemed perfectly content with the idea.

Something in Hudson's gut tightened a little at the sight of her with Eli. Long-ago dreams of a family with Ava pushed to the surface, and his heart did a little skip at the thought. They'd been so young, still discovering their feelings for each other then. If he were completely honest with himself, though, he'd been in love with Ava since the first day Quinn brought her home and hailed her as the best nurse ever for fixing up her scraped knee at school.

She had always been strong, determined, and ready to stand up for the underdog. It didn't surprise him at all that Ava spent her life creating families from broken hearts and seemingly helpless situations.

She glanced up at him, smiling. "He looks like you."

"He does not."

Ava stepped closer. "He has your eyes."

As if he knew they were discussing his features, Elijah cooed at them.

"He also has your smile. At least the way I remember it being. It's been such a long time since I've seen you truly smile."

Hudson frowned. "I smile. When I have a reason."

"And this little guy isn't reason enough? I'm positive now that he's Quinn's son. That letter was written by her, and she *is* alive."

A tiny little part of him hoped she was right, but all logic and nearly a decade of police work said she just couldn't be. Not to mention, admitting she was right meant he had been wrong and so angry all those years for nothing. Hudson hated admitting he was wrong about little things, but this? This meant his sister was alive and possibly not that far away, and he never once looked for her. He let her be gone and maybe in danger for a decade. How could he live with that?

"No, Ava. You're seeing things because you want to see them. Quinn has been gone for over ten years."

She stared up at him, her expression giving away nothing about what she had to be feeling. He hated so much that his words hurt her, but how could he just abandon all he'd thought to be true for so long on Ava's gut feeling? He met her stare with his own. They stood that way for too long, each with so much to say and no way to put it into words.

"There are things you don't know about your sister, Hudson. Things she didn't want you to know."

"Are y'all okay?" Sandy stood across the room eyeing them.

Crap. He'd forgotten she was there.

Ava turned away from him. They would definitely be revisiting Quinn's secrets as soon as they got out of the group home.

"We're fine. Thanks." He cleared his throat, annoyed at the interruption. "I need a photo of the baby for the missing person's report. I didn't get one earlier."

Sandy gave a curt nod. "Go ahead."

He pulled his cell phone from his pocket and snapped a quick picture of Eli, his cute little face tugging at Hudson's heartstrings.

"Thanks so much, ma'am." He motioned toward Sandy. "Ava, give Elijah back."

Her eyes glossed over with unshed tears. He could practically hear her heart break as she handed the baby back. "You sure were right about him. He is a little heartbreaker. That smile will melt icebergs and sink ships one day."

Sandy disappeared with the baby, and they showed themselves to the door. As they walked back to the truck, Ava stayed quiet. Once inside the cab, she remained that way. Hudson found her silence unsettling.

"I bet if you pulled out some baby pictures of you and Quinn, you'd see that Eli looks just like both of you. The Pierce genetics are strong, and he's already working the Pierce Smolder."

He glanced over at her, wishing he could be as confident as she was but knowing it was nothing more than misplaced hope that Quinn had actually been alive all along. "The Pierce Smolder? What is that?"

Ava sighed. "The ability to melt a heart with his eyes."

He had no idea how to reply, so a subject change seemed in order. "At least no one asked why you were with me. I didn't have to use the illegal adoptions cover story."

"Thank God for small miracles." She let out a huge yawn. "Can you take me home? I'm exhausted."

That was the last place he'd be taking her. "I told you earlier, I don't think you should go home. Yesterday, your house *and* your office were broken into. They'll be watching and waiting for you."

"Where am I supposed to go, then?" Defeat almost outranked anger in her voice. "We don't even know *who* they are or what they want. I can't avoid my life forever!"

"My place, like I said. It's getting to be near dinnertime. We'll make something to eat. You can sleep in my guest room, and tomorrow we can make a better plan." He turned down the side street that led to his house without waiting on her reply.

"I *am* really hungry. It's been forever since I've eaten." Ava leaned her head back against the seat. "I don't have any other option right now, do I?"

"I promise we will figure it all out, just not tonight."

She sat straight up again. "They never tried to actually hurt me."

He pulled the truck up in front of his house and shut the engine off before turning to face her. "How about the shot they took at you through the window of your office?"

"Maybe it wasn't even the same people."

Hudson shook his head. He could tell she didn't believe herself. "When they broke into your office, you could have been seriously hurt... or worse."

"But I wasn't." Ava crossed her arms over her chest.

"Only because they didn't find you."

SIX

"ONLY BECAUSE THEY DIDN'T FIND YOU."

Ava shivered as Hudson's words hit home. There was no way to deny the danger—it would just be nice if she understood it. Why were strange men after her? She hadn't done anything—that she knew of, anyway—to make anyone angry. The only thing that made even a tiny bit of sense was the baby. The break-in at her office and their mention of "the boss" seemed so surreal, yet her missing laptop and torn-apart files were very tangible.

Hudson poked her thigh lightly, pulling her out of her thoughts. "Are you okay?"

Was she okay? No. Probably not. She undid her seat belt. "I'm fine. It's just all... so much, you know?"

"I know, and I'm sorry."

"And with it being the anniversary of Quinn's disappearance—of all the days for a baby to show up —and... and everything else."

The mention of his sister seemed to hit Hudson straight in the heart. "No matter what I do or how much time passes, I just can't seem to get past it."

Surprised at his admission, she could tell he tried not to flinch when Ava reached over and placed her hand on top of his. Touching him felt so familiar, increasing the ache in her heart when she dared think of all the time that had come between them.

Ava ran a finger softly across the back of his hand. "We were kids. Why wouldn't we believe the police? You know now how those things work. Would you have done anything differently if you had been an investigator back then?"

He shook his head and pulled his hand away to run his fingers through his hair.

After undoing his seat belt, he reached for the door handle. "No. Probably not. The currents were rough, so drowning made sense. And nothing ever gave a hint of any other outcome."

Ava yawned so hard, her body trembled. Clapping a hand over her mouth, she let out a little laugh. "I guess I'm pretty tired."

"It's been a long two days. Let's get inside and

make some food. You can shower, then get some shut-eye. It's always easier to figure things out in the daylight." Hudson pushed open the truck door and exited the vehicle.

She did the same, still wondering how she'd ended up stuck with the one man who had never wanted to see her ever again.

Until a baby she just knew had to be her best friend's child had shown up in church, Ava had enjoyed her quiet, uneventful life. Even if sometimes she was a bit lonely, her work kept her busy and happy. Hudson had made it abundantly clear at Quinn's funeral service that she was no longer welcome in his life, and she had accepted that, even if it had been incredibly painful. Hopefully, they could find her a different place to stay in the morning so they wouldn't be forced to be so civil to each other. Even though it went unmentioned, the tension surrounding them was so palpable it felt oppressive.

As she followed Hudson to the front door, she glanced around at the quiet neighborhood. A long row of beach-style cottages just like hers spread out on either side of the street. A few porch lights burned along it, but mostly it was dark and peaceful. It was the same as her own neighborhood and most of the others in their hometown. Sunrise had always been a peaceful place. The only outsiders it drew in were the few vacationers who preferred to avoid the busy tourist destinations of the Outer Banks. Never in a million years had she expected anything like what had been happening in the last day or so.

Once inside, he led the way to a small bedroom toward the back of the house. Gesturing through the doorway, he kept his distance from her. "This is the guest room. You're the only guest I've ever had, though, so I have no idea if the bed is comfortable or not."

She gave him a small smile as she entered the room. "Thank you, Hudson. I promise to get out of your hair tomorrow. I know this hasn't been easy for you."

He shrugged and kicked at the doorframe lightly. "I'm just doing my job."

"No. You have gone above and beyond, just like you always have. I know how hard this is for you because it's making my heart ache too. I appreciate it, though—more than I can say. Despite what I said earlier, I couldn't imagine sleeping in my house tonight. Not while the window is gone and those men know where I live. And work."

Hudson grunted. She couldn't be sure, but it seemed like his eyes had gotten a little moist. "I'm going to get you something to sleep in." He walked away, disappearing into the next open doorway.

Ava set her purse on the dresser and looked around. A queen-sized wrought iron bed that she recognized as her long-lost best friend's sat against one wall. A nightstand was beside the bed, and she noted an open door to a bathroom. She definitely needed a hot shower.

A light tap on the door caught her attention. Hudson stood there, holding out a T-shirt and a pair of running pants. "This is the best I could do. They'll probably be too big."

Smiling, she accepted his offerings. "I'm sure they're just fine. Thank you."

He shifted his weight, leaning into the doorframe. "Okay, well, let me know if you need anything. The bathroom has everything you need for a shower. There are even extra toothbrushes in the cabinet below the sink."

"Thank you." Reaching out, she placed a hand on his arm. "I know this is weird for you. I appreciate you letting me stay."

Hudson shrugged. "It's no big deal. As long as you're safe. I know Quinn would want me to keep you safe." Turning, he walked away, disappearing again into the other bedroom.

She glanced around the tidy space that was oddly feminine for a room in a bachelor pad. Several framed photos stood on the dresser. One of them was of Hudson and Quinn as babies, smiling up at the camera. She'd forgotten how close in age they were. Ava picked up the frame and ran her finger along the outline of her best friend and her first love. She thought of Eli and how convinced she was that he belonged to Quinn.

"I just know your mama is alive, little man," she murmured. "Your mama and my best friend. We both just need to prove it. And I promise you, we will."

She set the picture back on the dresser and her phone on the nightstand by the bed. Quinn just had to be alive. And there had to be a darn good reason why she hadn't come home for all these years. She'd never have left Hudson so long if she didn't have to. In her heart, Ava believed that finding Eli was the biggest clue ever to locating Quinn.

Later, after a long-overdue shower and a quick dinner of spaghetti and meatballs with Hudson, Ava lay in bed, staring at the shadows on the ceiling. Semi-sheer curtains allowed the moonlight to cast eerie shapes from the trees outside the window across the room. Memories melded with the events of the past couple days, forming shadows in her mind that mimicked the ones in the room. She fell asleep with the image of Eli looking up at her with her best friend's blue eyes.

Despite the sheer exhaustion that had claimed her, Ava woke up early the next morning with a growling stomach and an intense need for hot coffee. The borrowed clothes hung loose and still smelled a little like Hudson. She liked that more than she probably should. When she tucked her phone into one of the pockets, the oversized pants sagged uncomfortably. Reluctant to take them off and put on her own dirty clothes again, she tightened the string in the waist, slipped her feet into her shoes, and padded to the bathroom. She washed her face with some warm water, then used the toothbrush she'd located the night before and cleaned her teeth. After finger-combing her hair, she tucked it behind her ears and headed out to rustle up some coffee in the kitchen.

She didn't have to work too hard. The heavenly scent of already brewing coffee drew her in. Hudson sat at the little table, drinking a cup and reading the paper.

"Good morning," she said, noting the mug that sat on the counter beside the coffee maker. "Okay if I use this cup?"

He looked up from the paper and nodded. His

gaze seemed appreciative of her wearing his clothing, but the vibe was extremely brief, and he said nothing about it. "Morning. I left it there for you."

"Thanks."

While she busied herself pouring the coffee and seeking cream from the refrigerator, Hudson got up and left the room. Trying not to feel a little hurt, she told herself he'd be right back and hadn't left because of her. Even when he didn't actually return.

As she took a sip of the coffee, she breathed in deeply. The taste was as amazing as the smell. A loud crash in another room made her drop the mug. It shattered, splashing the hot liquid everywhere.

She ran to the entryway and shouted toward the front of the house, "Hudson! What's going on? Are you okay?"

Pounding footsteps filled the small home, followed by shouting and a series of gunshots.

They'd found her again!

She ran toward the noise but froze when she caught sight of the mess in the living room. Overturned furniture, papers strewn everywhere, and a broken lamp littered the space. The front door stood open, so she ran to it and peered out but saw nothing. More crashing and shouting filled the house. She ran back toward the noise and spotted Hudson engaged in a fight with two men.

"Ava! Run! Get out of here!" Hudson's strained voice bellowed over the rest of the chaos. She spotted him in the dining room that sat adjacent to the living room.

Instead of doing as he said, she froze, torn between saving herself and making sure Hudson he was okay. He yelled at her again. *"Go!"*

Turning away from the shouting and constant crashing as furniture was upended and things were broken, she ran out the back door and through the lush garden space until she broke through the tree line and onto some dunes. Several hundred yards ahead of her lay the ocean. To the right and left were empty beaches. For a brief second, she wished they lived in the crowded tourist areas of the Outer Banks so there'd be more hiding places. Looking for some-where—anywhere—to hide, she spun 180 degrees, scanning the entire area. To the left, she spotted a life-guard's stand—the kind with an actual cabin for storage on it. Given its ramshackle appearance, it had likely long since been abandoned in favor of the new ATVs and such the guards used now and was only used for storage.

The shouting got louder. The intruders must have

followed her out the back door. Ava ran with everything she had toward the old wood structure.

Please let that shack be open.

Her shoes filled with sand, and the drooping pants weighed her down, but she pressed on. Why hadn't she run in another direction to a neighbor's house or even into the middle of the street? The sand was making it so hard to get away.

After what felt like forever, she made it to the base of the stand. Running up the ramp, she yanked at the door, and it opened with no resistance. Pulling the door closed behind her, she then climbed around dust-covered lifesaving equipment, battered cardboard boxes, and what was probably a rat running over her toes. Thank goodness she'd slipped her shoes on before leaving the bedroom. Enough light penetrated the spaces between the old boards to aid her. Burying herself deep in the mess, she waited.

It didn't take long for the voices of her pursuers to reach her.

"Where'd she go?" one guy asked.

"There's not much to choose from out here," another man answered. "I don't see her in the water."

"Look!" the first guy shouted. "She went this way!"

"You sure?" the other one answered.

"See? She left us a trail. I bet she's in the old shack over there!"

Her footprints! She totally forgot the fact that she'd just left her pursuers a trail of solid breadcrumbs right to her hiding spot. Glancing around her for anything she could use as a weapon, she spotted the outline of what looked like a small hatch in the floor.

Footsteps pounded up the ramp, and then the door crashed open against the wall of the shack. A large shadow blocked the sunlight coming in from the newly opened door.

"She's gotta be in here."

Ava grabbed the latch and pushed the hatch door down, opening a narrow space in the floorboards. As the two men shoved boxes and things out of the way, she dropped down through the hole into the sand below and took off running back toward the dunes and the trees beyond.

Without stopping to see if anyone was following her yet, she drew on every bit of the energy reserves she had left as she ran toward the trees. Breaking through the line into the wooded area, she let out a scream as a large form stepped in front of her and wrapped his arms around her.

"Let me go!" She stomped her foot down on one of her captor's feet, making him groan.

A hand clapped over her mouth. She tried to bite the fingers but couldn't get enough purchase.

A voice next to her ear stopped her flailing. "Will you stop struggling? It's me, Ava!" Hudson. It was only Hudson.

She instantly stopped, and he uncovered her mouth. "Shhh, they'll hear you."

"Who are these men, Hudson? What do they want from me? It's all too much." Ava sucked in air, trying to fill her burning lungs. Her entire body shook as yet another burst of adrenaline coursed through her body.

He grabbed her hand and tugged, leading her through trees and into someone's backyard. "We need to get out of here. They're probably right behind us."

Running with him through the yard to the front of the house, she spotted his truck three driveways down.

"We need to get to the truck. Can you keep up?" he asked, still pulling her along.

"Yes! Just go!"

They sprinted the rest of the distance to the truck before jumping in and backing out of the driveway just as their pursuers stepped into the street. A bullet pinged off the roof. Another hit the bumper as Hudson floored the gas pedal and took off.

"Are you okay?" he asked as he raced down the street.

"I'm fine." She sucked in a couple deep breaths. "Just out of breath." Ava buckled her seat belt and leaned against the seat as they sped all the way through town. Neither of them spoke for a few long minutes.

"They figured out where you lived too," she observed, finally breaking the tense silence.

Hudson gripped the steering wheel so hard, his knuckles turned white. His jaw ticked with the concentration he was exerting in order to stay on the road. "I know they did."

She sighed. "This is not good."

He glanced over at her quickly. "No. It's not."

He didn't say anything else, so neither did she.

WHAT HAD AVA GOTTEN INVOLVED IN? HE asked himself that very question over and over as he tore through town at breakneck speed, praying he wouldn't encounter any of his well-meaning colleagues trying to stop him. Over the span of just a few days, someone had destroyed Ava's house, ransacked her office, and shot at them in his home. None of it made any sense.

It had to be related to the baby. It had all started when little Elijah had shown up at the church. Part of him—a really large part, in fact—hoped it did have something to do with Quinn. What he couldn't do, though, was reconcile in his mind Quinn's involvement with men like the ones who had been after Ava.

It just didn't make any sense at all.

Ten years of missing his sister had been harder than losing his parents. He and Quinn had done everything together. So close in age, they could have been twins; losing her had torn a hole in his heart. The thought that she might actually be alive and hadn't come home was just too much to think about.

He shook his head as he drove, as if to drive the hope away. He *knew* Quinn had died out there in the ocean. The case had closed long ago. He had to stop going down that road.

Still, those men chasing Ava meant business. And they had known where to find her. They knew to look at his house. How had they connected the two of them? Who had she pissed off? That was the biggest question.

He needed to sit down with Ava and really discuss

her most recent adoption placements as soon as he got them somewhere safe.

Glancing over at the woman beside him, he frowned. She was gripping the door handle tightly, and most of the color had left her already fair skin as she stared at the road ahead of them.

"Are you okay, Ava?"

She nodded but didn't say anything.

In the rearview mirror, he caught sight of a dark sedan closing the distance between them much too quickly. The hit men had caught up with them.

Think, Pierce! Where can you go?

Hudson made a sharp turn onto a country road, kicking the back wheels of his truck out to the left and raising a cloud of dust all around them. Having grown up in the area, he knew the back roads as well as he did his own reflection.

When the dust settled, he could see that the sedan had made the turn and still pursued them.

"Hang on!" he shouted as he floored the gas pedal and the truck shot forward, leaving their pursuers far behind them. In about half a mile, there would be an old hiking trail in the state park that led to the dunes by the bay. He used to follow it when he spent hours wandering the park after Quinn first disappeared. If he remembered correctly, it would be just wide enough to fit the truck if he didn't get stuck in the sand.

The speedometer maxed out at 120 as he gripped the wheel as hard as possible. Ava stayed quiet, practically crushing the door handle and staring straight ahead. As he passed a small swampy area filled with lily pads, one of the tires slipped off the edge of the road.

Holding tight, he steadied the truck and plowed forward, hoping no other cars would be in the oncoming lane when he had to make the turn. Their luck ran out when he spotted an oversized SUV coming toward them at what appeared to be a leisurely speed. In exactly thirty seconds, he needed to make a hard left across the oncoming lane and onto the narrow trail. If the SUV didn't speed up, it would block his turn, and they'd have nowhere left to hide from their pursuers.

"They're in the way!" Ava shouted.

As the distance closed between their truck and the turn, Hudson sent up one long prayer begging for the SUV to move. Instead of speeding up, it slowed down.

Hudson maintained their speed, trying to calculate how far past the turn he could get and still make it. "Don't worry, Ava—I've got this!"

As if the driver of the SUV heard his silent pleas, they suddenly sped up and roared past. Half a second later, Hudson jerked the wheel left and headed straight to the wooded area across the road.

"We're going to crash!" Ava yelled, covering her eyes with her hands.

They plowed through the overgrown brush and into the treed area. Seconds later they hit sand, and the truck slowed quickly, sending them both flying forward toward the dashboard. Ava smacked her forehead hard and fell limp against the door. The wheels spun as he continued to flatten the gas pedal to the floor.

"Come on!" He slapped a palm against the steering wheel just as the truck tires found purchase, and the vehicle jerked forward again. He pulled through the grassy dunes. When he made it to the hard-packed, wet sand, he turned the truck and headed toward the only structure around. The city-owned pavilion wouldn't offer much protection, but there might be a park ranger there who could help them.

Keeping one eye on the rearview mirror and the other on the target, Hudson sped across the empty beach. Pulling in on the far side of the building, he then shut the truck off and jumped out. As he ran for the passenger side, he called for help.

A man dressed in a park ranger's uniform appeared. "What's going on?"

"My friend is hurt!" He undid the seat belt that secured Ava and pulled her from the cab of the truck. Blood ran down from her temple to her chin.

"Bring her inside. We have first aid supplies." The ranger led him up several stairs and into the building.

Cold air assaulted Hudson as he entered, causing him to shiver. The heat and humidity outside seemed so much worse when compared to the air-conditioned environment.

"Over there." The ranger pointed. "Put her on that couch."

Hudson did as he was told, laying Ava gently against the cushions. When he turned to face the other man, he showed him the badge on his belt. "Detective Hudson Pierce. You must be new around here."

"Ranger Bobby Marlowe. I just moved to the area last week, actually. Nice to meet you. Now, what happened?"

"We were on a case when a vehicle began to pursue us. I hit sand and bottomed out. Ava hit her head on the dash. She had a seat belt on, but the jerking of the vehicle flung her forward. She's going to be bruised and achy later."

"With one heck of a headache." Bobby sat down on a small coffee table beside the couch and opened his first aid kit. Pulling out a bottle of hydrogen peroxide, he then soaked a four-by-four gauze pad and gently cleaned the wounded area. "Head wounds, even minor ones, always bleed so much. They look scary even when they're not."

Once the area was clean, Hudson could see that the cut was relatively minor, and he relaxed. Now if only Ava would wake up.

Bobby placed a couple small butterfly bandages over the wound. "She should be good to go as far as the head wound goes. But if she doesn't wake up soon, I'd say she needs a trip to the ER. She definitely needs to check in with her doctor. Any hit to the head that knocks someone out is going to have some consequences."

As he stood up and gathered his first aid supplies, Ava let out a little groan. Raising a hand, she pressed it to her forehead. "My head hurts."

Hudson took Bobby's spot on the coffee table. "You hit the dash pretty hard. It's no wonder it hurts."

She opened one eye and looked over at him. "Oh

yeah." She frowned. "I remember now. Did we make it? Where are we?"

He nodded. "We're at one of the aid stations in the park. Ranger Bobby here fixed your wound all up for you."

She turned her head slightly until she could see Bobby and gave a little wave. "Thanks. I appreciate it. I'd appreciate some ibuprofen even more, if you have any."

Bobby chuckled. "Why don't you see if you can sit up, and I'll get you some with a glass of water?"

Ava shifted on the sofa so her feet swung down to the floor and slowly lifted herself into an upright position.

Hudson frowned as he watched, wanting to scoop her up and run as far and as fast as he could from that place. Holding an unconscious Ava in his arms had done things to him—things he didn't want to examine at the moment. It was enough to be dealing with the firm knot in his gut that had formed when she'd first hit her head. The idea of another woman he cared about—

He shook his head to clear the thought. Caring about Ava was in the past. His only bronco in the rodeo now centered on finding out who wanted her —and why.

"Hey, you okay, man?" Bobby stood in front of him holding a bottle of pills and a glass of water.

Hudson turned his focus on the ranger. "Yeah. Fine. Just got lost in the details of our case for a minute."

Ava reached out and touched him, her fingers light on his arm. "We're going to figure this out. I just know it."

He stood and stepped out of her reach. "I'm just glad you're not seriously hurt."

Bobby handed Ava the glass of water and a couple of the ibuprofen tablets.

"Thank you." She took a long drink of water with the pills.

Hudson's cell phone rang in his pocket. A quick glance at the screen showed the number for the social worker, Janet James.

"Pierce here." He walked across the room and stood by a large window that looked out over the ocean.

"Detective Pierce? This is Janet James."

She sounded upset. The knot in his gut tightened. "What's wrong, Ms. James?'

"It's Elijah. I just got a call from the group home."

"Is he okay?" he interrupted, raising his voice louder than he meant to.

Ava jumped off the couch. "What happened to Eli?"

He raised his pointer finger to tell her to wait a minute as Janet explained.

"Apparently two men showed up at the home early this morning, demanding to have Elijah. Said they were his uncles and that their sister wanted him back.

"Of course, no one let them in, but they raised quite a fuss and promised to be back later with 'reinforcements,' whatever that means. I doubt they were referring to an attorney. Maybe the mother had a change of heart and wanted to circumvent the courts to get her baby back?"

"I don't think so, Ms. James." Hudson continued to look down at the ocean. The waves below looked so peaceful; he could hardly comprehend the storm his life had become.

She sighed. "I don't either. That's why I called you. Something is very wrong with this entire situation."

"Don't worry. I'll head over there and check in on everything."

"I was hoping you'd say that. I don't know why, but I'm just really worried. Thank you, Detective. I'll meet you there." She ended the call before he could say anything else.

Janet showing up there was a very bad idea. He felt it in his gut. Stowing his phone in the pocket of his jeans, he turned to Ava. "We've gotta go."

The fear he'd felt hearing Janet's announcement was mirrored in Ava's features. "Is Eli okay?"

"So far. But we really need to get over there." He turned to Bobby. "Thank you for your amazing first aid skills."

Bobby nodded. "I'm just glad I was here to assist. This is more excitement than I've ever had on a shift. If you need anything else, I'm here."

"Watch your back, man. I don't know who these guys are, but if they show up here, you never saw us." Hudson really hoped they hadn't led the men there, but anything was possible at that point.

"Got it," Bobby replied.

They shook hands once more, and then Hudson waved Ava toward the door. "Let's go."

"Thanks for fixing me up, Ranger Bobby." She gave him a quick hug before she followed Hudson out the door.

Once they were in the truck and headed down the beach, Ava turned to him. "Are you going to tell me what's going on now or what?"

"Two men showed up at Eli's group home this morning, claiming to be his uncles and that his mother wanted him back. When the workers refused to let them in, they promised to return later with reinforcements. I'm afraid that will mean more armed men."

She clapped a hand over her mouth. "No! We have to get him out of there!"

He nodded, his hands cramping from gripping the steering wheel so tightly. "We will. That's why we're going there now. No one is taking that baby. Especially until I know for a fact that he isn't Quinn's."

SEVEN

Ava could hear the solid conviction in Hudson's voice. It was the first time since Eli showed up at the church that he seemed to really believe Quinn could actually be alive.

"You mean you agree with me?"

"I don't know, Ava. I just don't know. The possibility goes against everything in me, but those men are after something. At first I was convinced it was you they wanted, but now that they've gone to the children's home... I just don't know what to believe."

Anxiety gripped her tighter than she held the door handle of the truck as Hudson broke a dozen different laws on his way back to the home.

"I wish we knew why these men were so interested in the baby. If—and that's a huge if— he is

Quinn's child, what has my sister been wrapped up in all these years?"

The truck hit a bump hard, causing her to bounce up out of the seat. The sudden fast motion made her super woozy from her previous head injury. She reached up and touched the bandages on her temple.

"Sorry about that," Hudson said, keeping his eyes on the road ahead of them. "I'll try to be more careful."

She could see the outline of a vein on the side of his neck as all the muscles pulled taut. He knew as well as she did that Eli was not only in trouble but also the key to finding out what had happened to Quinn. "Don't worry about me. Just get there."

"I need to call this in. Can you hand me my phone?" He pointed at the floor where his phone had somehow ended up. "We're going to need backup."

Ava reached down and grabbed his phone, then handed it to Hudson. He hit a button, and the call went straight through to the police department. He gave a quick update to whoever answered before dropping his phone in the little well of the console.

"A couple marked cars will meet us there."

"Good," she replied. The more cops who showed up, the better she'd feel.

It took less than ten minutes more for them to

reach the county group home. Hudson drove around back of the building, kicking up dust and gravel as he barely slowed the vehicle.

"Why are we back here?" Ava asked.

He slammed on the brakes, the momentum jarring her aching head once more, and put the truck in Park. "Tactics. If they pull in up front, they won't know we're here." He turned the key to kill the engine. "You good?"

She nodded as she undid her seat belt. "Yes."

They both jumped from the truck, and she let Hudson lead the way back around to the front door. Definitely in cop mode, he stayed close to the building, gun drawn and hypervigilant of their surroundings. Ava just let him do his thing as she followed along, scanning the property around them. She'd never been a cop, but she'd taken more than one self-defense class that warned her to always have situational awareness.

They made it to the front corner closest to the road. Hudson, moving slowly, shifted his position around to the front, glancing all around the yard and driveway to make sure it was empty before gesturing for her to join him.

They could see two police cruisers headed toward

them from down the road. Hudson waved them around the building. Both drivers complied.

"Come on." He led the way to the front door, his head basically on a swivel as he assessed the area around them while they moved.

Hudson pounded on the heavy wooden door. When no one responded, he rang the doorbell over and over. Finally, the door opened, and the older woman they'd met the last time appeared, fear bright in her eyes. Two uniformed officers had joined them.

She clapped a hand to her mouth. "Oh thank God, it's just y'all."

"Is the baby safe?" Hudson demanded.

The woman nodded. Visibly shaken by the earlier visitors, she just kept repeating, "Thank you, Lord," over and over.

"Is anyone here right now?" Hudson asked.

She shook her head.

"Okay, good." He holstered his weapon, then locked the door, including the dead bolt. "I doubt this will stop them, but at least we'll have a few seconds' warning." He pointed out the kitchen and the hallway to the other two officers. "Can one of you cover each of those areas?"

"Got it, Detective." The younger of the two headed

toward the service entrance in the kitchen. "No one will get by me."

The older officer just gave a nod and disappeared down the hall.

"What's down there?" Hudson asked the woman.

"Bedrooms mostly. One emergency exit at the end. I don't understand any of this." She ran her fingers through short, wild curls. "Usually babies come here because no one wants them. This is the total opposite. Why is this baby so important to them?"

Ava stepped aside as Hudson directed the upset woman to a chair in the corner of the room. "I wish I could tell you, ma'am. All I can say is he is essential to a current investigation. I'm really sorry that it put you in a scary position."

She leaned back against the chair and covered her eyes with a hand. "He's just a baby. How could he be essential to anything having to do with those horrible men?"

Every little sound made Ava jump, expecting armed men to burst through the front door at any moment. The little tic at the side of Hudson's jaw told her he felt the same way.

He walked to a window and looked through the curtains. "Where is the baby now, ma'am?"

The woman looked over at him. "What?'

"The baby," Ava said. "Where is he?"

She waved a hand in the direction of the hallway. "In the nursery."

"You go find him," Hudson told Ava as he peered through the curtains again. "I'll keep an eye out."

"Okay." She hurried away, disappearing down the hall. For a children's home, it seemed eerily quiet once again.

Passing several open doors, she peered into each one, only to find empty rooms beyond. At the end of the hall, a door stood partially open, and the strains of a lullaby drifted softly toward her. Through the opening, she saw several cribs lined up against one wall. A brightly colored throw rug sat in the center of the room with little fabric bins full of toys distributed across it. Off to one side, a woman about Ava's age sat in a rocking chair, holding an infant. When she saw Ava, she held a finger to her lips.

Ava nodded and stepped into the room, moving quietly.

"Elijah?" she whispered.

The woman pointed to the crib closest to her. "He's sleeping," she whispered back, distrust darkening her features. "Who are you?"

"I'm with the police department. We're going to take him into protective custody."

The woman stood up, shifting the baby she held to her shoulder and moving between Ava and the crib holding Eli. "Do you have a badge and identification?"

Ava smiled at her, trying to win the other woman's trust. She obviously took her duty to her little charges very seriously. "No. I'm not a cop. I just work with the department. I'm an adoption agent."

"Elijah will be staying right here, then, until a police officer with proper credentials comes for him."

"Please." Ava took a couple steps forward. "I need to get him out of here before those men come back."

As if on cue, several vehicles pulled into the parking lot in front of the building, engines racing and tires squealing. Ava ran to a window and peeked out. At least six men had exited the vehicles and were gathered near the three dark-colored sedans that had just arrived. Two of them had rifles slung across their chests.

She turned back to the protective caregiver. "I really need to get him out of here. *Now.*"

The woman shook her head. "I'm sorry, but I can't do that."

The woman who had let them in suddenly appeared in the doorway, her eyes wild with fear. "Let her take him! She's with the police. They're going to protect him."

"We can't!" The second woman tried to put herself between Ava and Eli's crib.

"I will take the blame! If they don't get him out of here, we might all be hurt. Or worse!" She turned to Ava, her expression saturated with fear. "Take the boy! Get him out of here!"

Several loud booms reverberated as someone pounded on the front door, the shocking sound jarring them both. One of the babies began to cry. A few seconds later, another baby joined the first one.

A dozen crazy-loud pops filled the air, each one coming in quick succession to the one before. Someone was shooting at the building. Two more babies started crying.

She heard Hudson yelling for her. "Ava! Where are you? Get Elijah and come on! We have to get out of here right *now*!"

Ava pushed past the woman and ran to the crib where she found Elijah. Reaching down, she picked him up and held him to her chest. "Does he have a diaper bag or anything?"

More pounding followed by several more gunshots and the sound of breaking glass filled the house.

"Oh my God! The children!" the younger woman sobbed in the middle of the room.

The older woman grabbed a bag from a nearby changing table. Shoving diapers, wipes, some baby sleepers, and a can of formula with a couple bottles into it haphazardly, she held it out to Ava. "Go! And take those men with you!"

Ava could see the fear in her eyes and hear it in her voice. "Thank you! Block the door with anything you can, and stay down!" She snatched the bag and ran from the room toward the main living room and Hudson. As she made it to the end of the hall, she caught sight of Hudson, his gun drawn and aimed at the front door.

With his free hand, he tossed her the keys to his truck. "Get out of here, Ava! Find another way to get to the truck and leave!"

She caught the keys, clutching Eli to her chest, where panic held her tight. "I'm not leaving you, Hudson!"

"I'll call you when I can! Just go! Take the back door in the kitchen—Brown's in there. He'll cover you. Once you're in the truck, call 9-1-1 and head straight to the police precinct."

She hesitated for half a second, her heart begging her not to leave Hudson, but her mind knew what she had to do. "Be careful! Please!"

More gunshots hit the door with incredible force,

several splintering the wood. Something heavy slammed against the door next, the boom echoing through the space.

"Go, Ava!"

Turning, she ran full force across the room and pushed through the closed door that led to the kitchen. Plowing through the wide-open space, she slipped and slid across the tiles. The front door flew open behind her, accompanied by angry voices. Ava pushed forward, trying not to think about Hudson and what was happening in the other room.

"Miss! Where are you going?" Officer Brown reached for her, but she dodged out of the way.

"I've got to get Eli to the police precinct. Hudson said to have you cover me."

The officer looked shocked and a little confused, but he nodded. "Do you need me to drive you?"

"No." Ava gasped for air. Her lungs burned as adrenaline saturated every cell in her body. "I just need to get out of here so you can go back up Hudson."

Brown nodded once more.

Grasping the knob, she turned it and yanked the back door open. Running as fast as she could with a crying Eli and his bag in her arms, she clicked the key fob to unlock the truck. When she slid into the driver's seat, she tossed the diaper bag aside, then jammed the key into the ignition and turned it, half expecting bullets to rain down all over the truck. When there were no gunshots in her direction, Ava exhaled the breath she hadn't realized she'd been holding.

Eli continued to sob, his cries breaking her heart.

"I'm so sorry, little man. Everything is going to be fine, though, I promise. I just need to get us out of here."

After the truck roared to life, she put it into gear, and, using one hand to drive and the other to hold the baby, she floored the gas pedal and roared out of the yard. Dirt, grass, and gravel kicked up in a cloud that surrounded her until she made the turn to the front of the building. Eli let out a loud howl that made her ears hurt. With speeds that should have gotten her license taken away, Ava sped down the drive toward the main road.

Please just let us get away.

As she drove, she repeated the thought over and over. Checking the rearview mirror repeatedly and continuing to press the pedal to the floor, she drove straight into the center of town and pulled into the police department parking lot. Heading around the side of the building that wasn't visible to the road, she parked under a tree and turned the truck off.

She'd forgotten to call 9-1-1.

Surprisingly, as the truck went quiet, so did the baby.

"You okay there, buddy?" Ava pushed the driver's seat back so she could loosen her grip on Eli. He looked up at her with clear blue eyes, big, salty drops of tears clinging to his long lashes. She swore she could see Quinn in his features. "It's going to be okay. We're gonna find your mama, I promise."

Laying Eli down on the passenger seat, she reclined the seat so he could nestle in the little dip formed where the two parts of it met. She watched for a moment as Eli shoved his little fist in his mouth and sucked contentedly. Next, she fished her cell phone from her purse and called the emergency number. Her pulse pounded loudly in her ears as her heart slammed around in her chest. Ava took a deep, steadying breath as the call rang through.

"9-1-1. What's your emergency?"

"This is Ava Taft. I'm an adoption worker who was consulting with Detective Pierce on the baby found in the church."

"How can I help you, ma'am? You do realize this is an emergency line, right?"

Her hands began to shake from the adrenaline rush clearing away. She gripped the phone a little tighter. "Would you consider a shoot-out at the county children's home where Detective Pierce and two other officers desperately need backup an emergency?"

The line filled with static, then went dead. She tossed her phone on the seat beside in her in frustration. Hopefully, the operator was sending help.

She glanced around the parking lot. Not feeling safe or secure, Ava decided it best to go inside. She gathered her purse, the diaper bag, and Eli and headed to the door of the precinct. Maybe someone in there could get help to Hudson.

The lobby was empty. Even the desk sergeant was missing. Taking yet another chance that could get her in a lot of trouble, she slipped down the hallway to the office she now knew to be Hudson's. Closing the door, she then turned the lock. The building was still eerily quiet. She stood with her back to the door for a full minute until the distant sound of a flushing toilet caught her ear. Footsteps headed in the direction of the front desk echoed in the hall.

Ava relaxed some. Settling into the big chair behind the desk with a sleepy Eli nestled to her shoulder, she set her phone on the desk and waited.

Five minutes passed. *Where are you?*

Then ten. *Come on, Hudson. Call me!*

Please let him be okay. I can't lose him again. Not like this.

She could feel her pulse pounding in her neck as her heart raced the Indy 500 in her chest. Finally, after twenty minutes, the phone rang with Hudson's number on the screen.

"Are you okay?" she asked instead of saying hello.

"Yeah. Where are you now?" He sounded out of breath.

"At the police station, in your office."

"Okay, good."

"Did they leave the group home?" Ava asked.

Hudson took a deep breath, then exhaled heavily. "Thankfully yes. I wasn't sure if they would, but once they figured out my truck was gone, they took off. I'm guessing they're on the hunt for you and Eli, so I want you to stay right where you are. I'll come to you."

"How will—"

The call dropped before she could finish asking *how* he'd get to them when the distance was more than five miles away.

She looked down at the baby she still held. Eli had fallen to sleep, his tiny fist shoved in his perfect little mouth. Her heart fluttered a bit. She'd never really thought much about having a baby herself. Placing babies with families who would love them as their own had been her life's mission. It never actually occurred to her that maybe one day she'd like to be a forever family to a child.

Yeah, she knew single women could adopt and all that. Ava had just always had this vision of a husband and a white picket fence around her yard when the time came to be a mother. And since she didn't have the husband, the rest had just sort of faded away.

Sighing, she leaned against the chair back and closed her eyes. Hopefully, Hudson would get there quickly, and they could find somewhere safe to go until they figured the whole mess out.

Eli cooed in his sleep. Ava smiled at the sweet sound. Whatever else had happened since Sunday, he made it all okay.

Hudson waved the patrol car down, relieved not to have to walk the rest of the way. The other two cops had agreed to stay on the scene for the workup. He'd waited for the crime scene team to arrive, then ducked out with the promise of returning after he ensured Ava and the baby were safe.

"Hey, man. You look like something my cat dragged in." The rookie patrol officer, Mike Samuels, gestured to the passenger seat. "Hop in, Detective."

Hudson didn't need to be asked twice. Jogging around the vehicle, he pulled open the passenger door and slid inside. "Can you take me to the station?"

"Sure thing." Samuels made a U-turn in the road and headed back the way he'd come. "What happened to you?"

"Nothing worth talking about. I called in a home invasion at the group home. Did you hear it go out over the radio?" Okay, so maybe it was Ava who had called it in, but what did it matter?

Samuels nodded. "Yeah. They sent units 4323 and 4325. Why did you leave? Where's your patrol unit?"

Hudson sighed. "I wasn't technically on duty. The woman in charge called me, scared by a couple of nasty-looking dudes who had threatened her over one of the babies."

"From a case?" They pulled up to a stoplight. "Was it the abandoned baby case from the weekend?"

"Yeah."

The light turned green. Samuels hit the gas, and they pulled through the intersection.

"I didn't know you were still working on that one. I thought Child Protective Services took over."

Hudson had no interest in answering any more questions, so he tried to shut down the rest of the third degree. "I'm actually on vacation this week. She just had my number, so she called me first."

They reached the police station. Samuels pulled the car up in front of the building. Hudson didn't see his truck anywhere, but then he remembered Ava said she was inside. Hopefully, she'd left it out back where it couldn't be seen from the road. He pushed open the door, then stepped out of the car. "Thanks for the lift, Samuels."

"No problem, Detective. I hope they find those guys. It takes a real piece of work to pull that stunt on a house full of little kids."

Hudson gave him a little salute of thanks, and then Samuels pulled away. After the car had left the lot, he jogged around back, relieved beyond measure to see his truck sitting in the lot, parked under a tree. He ran toward the building, pulled open the door, and went straight to his office. What he found inside stopped him in his tracks. Ava sat in his desk chair with her eyes closed, leaning back against the head-rest. Eli lay on her shoulder, also sound asleep. His chest tightened a little as he studied her. They were so young when he fell in love with Ava. That day on the beach when Quinn disappeared, he'd finally worked up the nerve to tell her how he felt. Five years he'd crushed on her, and that day was their first kiss.

He never quite got past the idea that his sister, the only family he had left in the world, had drowned while he and Ava were kissing under the pier.

Avoiding her for a decade hadn't been easy. Not in a town as small as Sunrise. With his parents gone—and Quinn—he'd basically become a hermit other than work. He'd convinced himself it was the penance he deserved for not being there to save his sister.

Spending time with Ava had begun to stir those old feelings he'd locked away so tightly, and that made him angry. Angry at himself for letting those feelings surface and angry at her for making it happen.

Anger he knew to be completely unjustified. It wasn't like Ava had dropped the baby at the church herself. Or sent armed men to destroy her home, office, and his home.

What they needed to do right then was find a safe place to go where Eli wouldn't be found, and then he could try to figure out if Quinn were somehow really connected to the baby like Ava thought. Maybe then he could figure out this thing with Ava. If there even was thing.

But first he needed to know who the men were who had been trying to get to Ava and why. His gut told him it all came back to the abandoned baby.

Ava opened her eyes and jumped when she caught sight of him. "You scared me! But I'm so glad you're okay. How did you get here so quickly?"

The relief in her eyes at seeing him tugged at his heart, making him even more annoyed at himself for letting her get under his skin.

"I grabbed a ride with a patrol car. Are you and the baby both okay?"

She smiled warmly. "We're both perfectly fine. Especially now that we know you're safe too."

The urge to kiss Ava came out of nowhere, but he quickly pushed it away. Taking a step back to put some physical distance between them, he took his cell phone from his pocket and pulled up the last two photos he'd taken. Showing the first one to Ava, he said, "I grabbed pictures of two of the guys. I'm going to go scan them and see if I can find any matches. Will you be okay here for a bit?"

He tried not to notice the hint of sadness that darkened her expression. "I could help you."

Hudson shook his head. "No. I don't want anyone

to recognize Eli. You need to stay in here. The ladies at the home are going to tell anyone who asks that he was taken during a home invasion. Which isn't entirely wrong. I've already notified my boss and the case manager of what really happened. We all agreed to keep it on the down-low to protect Eli. Janet said I could find somewhere safe to take him for a few days."

Ava tried to hide a little frown, but he caught it before she could. He sighed. Maybe leaving them alone wasn't such a great idea. What choice did he have, though? They needed to know who the men were so he'd know how to protect her and Eli.

"I'm glad everyone wants to keep him safe." She reached down and touched his little feet. "He's just so sweet."

It's not just the baby I need to keep safe.

Pushing that incriminating thought out of his mind, he gave her a partial smile. "I won't be long. I promise. It's probably better if we travel after dark anyway, since we don't have a car seat or anything."

She nodded. "Whatever you think is best."

He turned to walk away, but she called out to him, stopping him.

"What, Ava?"

"Aren't you supposed to actually be working? I

mean, you haven't gone to work since Sunday, and I don't want to get you fired trying to help me."

He kicked at an imaginary rock on the floor. "I'm technically on vacation. I always take this week off from work."

Hudson didn't wait for her to say anything else, just turned and strode away. He needed a little distance—fast.

It seemed like as much as he wanted to protect Ava, he also wanted to get away from her. So many confusing emotions had his mind in turmoil.

Why did she have to come back into my life? I was doing just fine alone.

Somewhere in the back of his brain, he could have sworn he heard someone say, *Were you really, though?*

He headed to one of the empty offices. He was one of only a handful of detectives in Sunrise, so he was lucky enough to have a private workspace, something he was keenly thankful for in that moment. Ava and Eli would likely go unnoticed because of it. The building seemed empty as he walked through it, which was something else to be thankful for.

Once he was settled at an unused computer, he emailed the photos to himself so he could upload them and compare them to a local database of known criminals. It didn't take long to get a match to one of them.

Pulling up the file, Hudson scanned it briefly. Creep number one had a multipage rap sheet with mostly organized-crime-related charges. As he read through the list, the second picture hit on the database. Creep number two had a shorter rap sheet but worse charges. Both men were involved with a local drug syndicate with ties to Central America, acting as security plus hit men. The local leader of the group, a man only referred to as "the boss" on both files, seemed to be a ghost.

Hudson ran his hand through his hair, exhaling hard. Things just got a whole heck of a lot more complicated with the local mob involved. Could Quinn really be wrapped up in this mess?

Did he just actually have that thought? Until that moment, he'd been 100 percent convinced she was dead, and nothing anyone could have said would change his mind.

Grabbing his phone, he scrolled through to the pictures of Eli. His brilliant blue eyes looked so much like Quinn's—and his own. How could he not have seen that earlier?

Was Quinn alive?

If she was, it would mean accepting that he'd let

her be dead for over a decade when he should have been searching for her. And how did Eli fit into any of this? There was no doubt he resembled the Pierce family. Or maybe he just saw that because he wanted to.

Letting out a long, frustrated sigh, Hudson closed his photo app and tried to come up with any other reason why the day someone had left a baby in the church just happened to coincide with the anniversary of when his sister supposedly drowned. And why that very same day, armed men had gone after Ava.

Printing both sheets, he logged out of the database, folded the papers, and tucked them into his pocket.

The sun had dropped below the horizon, casting long shadows over the parking lot and his truck. It was time to get Ava and Eli to safety.

He returned to his office and pushed the door open. Ava's eyes popped open as she jerked awake. She peered up at him from her reclined position, recognition not setting in right away. Instead fear and panic lit her up like a neon sign.

"Ava! It's just me!"

She stared at him as the panic slowly disappeared and recognition returned. "Hudson."

Worry clenched in his chest, even though he

knew nothing could have happened to them while locked in his office in the police building. "Are you okay?"

"Yeah. I guess I just dozed off for a minute. Did you find out anything useful?"

"I did. We need to get you somewhere safe first, and then I'll fill you in. How do you feel about sitting in the back seat with Eli? I feel like it would be somewhat safer."

She nodded. "Yes, I can definitely do that."

Ava stood up, careful not to disturb the baby still asleep in her arms. Even as disheveled as she was, with the moon behind her through the window, she looked absolutely beautiful. Without thinking, he reached up and tugged gently on one of her curls, just like he used to. "You know, you haven't changed a bit over the years."

A light flush, evident even in the dim lights of the precinct, traveled up her neck and over her cheeks. "You've always been a lousy liar, Hudson. I've changed far more than you'll even know."

She turned her attention to the sleeping baby, avoiding Hudson's gaze. "I'm sure little Eli's going to wake up absolutely starving any minute now."

He chuckled, letting her change the focus of their attention. "If Quinn is his mama and he's anything at all like her, he'll wake up hangry, not just hungry."

Ava laughed. "If that's not the absolute truth. Remember how she used to keep candy bars and snack cakes in her nightstand drawer in case she got hungry in the middle of the night?"

"It took me a good long time to empty that drawer after she disappeared. I guess I kept hoping she'd wake up hungry somewhere and come home to eat."

"Oh, Hudson. I can't even imagine what it was like for you."

He looked away, not wanting her to see the moisture threatening to fall from his eyes. "It's not like I gave you a chance to find out."

"I could have tried harder," she near whispered, then gave him a long look. "You do realize you just said that Quinn might be Eli's mother?"

"I do. I'm not saying I'm convinced. Something just keeps nagging at me that tells me I should I consider it." He patted the baby lightly on the back. "And this little guy sure does look a lot like her."

Ava smiled. "You finally see the resemblance. Good. I'll convince you yet, even if we need to run a DNA test at some point to prove it. We better get out of here now, though. I feel like it's only a matter of time until they show up here."

He nodded. "Yeah. You're probably right."

Once Ava and the baby were settled in the back seat, Hudson jumped in the truck and pulled out of the lot. Traffic almost nonexistent, it was easy for him to get out of the center of town quickly.

"Where are you taking us?" she asked, holding a still-sleeping Eli. "I swear this boy is a better sleeper than I am."

"I've got some friends who are off-grid. They'll help us. She's former NYPD, and he's a detective with his local town." He didn't mention they were located conveniently close to the last-known residences of both the guys who had been after them. If his gut feelings were right, and they usually were, those men would be headquartered near the "boss" mentioned in the files he'd read.

"Are you sure they won't mind us just dropping in on them?" She sounded genuinely worried.

"I'm positive. Once we get there, I'll fill you in on everything I just found out about the men chasing you and Eli."

Ava let out a long yawn. "Okay. Maybe I'll get to take a shower too. Do your friends have running water?"

Hudson couldn't stop the laughter. "Of course they do. Off-grid doesn't mean they live in a dirt hut.

It just means... well, it'll be better if you see it for yourself."

He could see her scowl in the rearview mirror. "You don't have to make fun of me."

"I swear I'm not." He bit back a second round of laughter. "It was just kinda cute. I haven't had much to laugh at in a long time. I'm sorry I made you feel bad."

She yawned again. "It's fine. I'm really tired. And probably extra sensitive too. I think I might close my eyes for a minute or two, if you don't mind?"

"Not at all. I'll let you know when we're close. It's about an hour's drive from here."

"Okay," she mumbled so quietly, he thought maybe she'd already begun to drift off.

EIGHT

"Ava? Wake up. We're here."

She opened one eye slowly, followed by the other. Forgetting for a moment where she was or what she'd been doing, the inside of Hudson's truck caught her off guard. Eli slept soundly in her arms where she was huddled in the corner of the seat near the door. At the opposite end of the bench seat, Hudson stood in the open door. Closing her eyes once more, she squeezed them tightly, then opened them once more. "I guess it wasn't all a dream."

"No." He shook his head. "Do you want to hand me the baby so you can get out and stretch a little? You've been curled up like that for over an hour."

"Yeah. Okay." She leaned over and handed Eli to him. The baby woke up and let out a little cry but immediately snuggled up against Hudson's shoulder. The sweet image made her briefly grieve for the future she used to think she'd have—with that man in particular.

She'd had so many dreams in those days. After Quinn disappeared, she'd stopped dreaming. The longer Hudson stayed away from her, the more hope she'd lost, until one day she'd simply accepted that there would be no fairy-tale ending for them.

Opening the door, she then stepped down from the truck into the darkness. What should have been complete silence instead held the sounds of hundreds of frogs and cicadas. Above it all, she made out the occasional hoot of an owl. Something buzzed her head as it flew by. The high-pitched sounds told her it was a bat. Waving her arms wildly to keep it away, she ran around the truck. As she made it to where Hudson stood, the area was suddenly drowned in the harshness of several floodlights. Ava raised an arm to cover her eyes.

"Who's out there?" a man called out.

"Logan! It's me, Pierce. Can you cut some of the lights off, please?"

The massive brightness disappeared, replaced only by a single light beside a large door. Someone stepped outside. "Hudson Pierce? What you doin' all the way out here in the middle of the night, man?"

Hudson exchanged a quick man hug with his friend as Ava stayed behind him. He still held Eli. She itched to take the baby back.

"I—we—need your help. You and Angie were the only ones I could think of."

"Of course! Come inside. I'll have Angie put on some coffee." He motioned them inside, stopping to lock the massive heavy door behind them with a series of dead bolts and latches. Ava followed Hudson down a hall to a huge open space.

"Hudson!" a petite woman with a pile of dark curls greeted them from the kitchen on the far side of the room.

"Hey, Angie. I'm sorry to drop in on you and Logan so late. I really had nowhere else to go."

"You know you're welcome here anytime. How are you?" She noticed Ava and the baby and stopped, smiling widely. "I see some things have changed since I saw you last."

Angie crossed the room and headed straight toward Ava. "Welcome! It's so nice to have you in our home...."

"Ava."

Angie stopped and looked at Hudson with a

hundred questions in her eyes. He just gave a little headshake. Ava frowned at the exchange as Angie turned her attention back to her.

"It's so nice to meet you, Ava. I'm Angie, and the big handsome man you met outside is the love of my life, Logan."

"You beckoned, darling?" Logan appeared by his wife's side, blue eyes sparkling as he leaned in and pressed a kiss to her cheek.

Angie gave him a little pat on the arm. "Just introducing you to our guest, since I'm 100 percent certain you didn't do it yourself. This is *Ava*."

The way the other woman said her name made Ava extremely uncomfortable.

"I planned to just as soon as I locked up," Logan said as he tried to hide his shock from her but failed miserably.

"It's obvious that you both know who I am. I'm not sure exactly what Hudson has told you about me, but he's made it abundantly clear that we're just trying to protect this little guy and that there is nothing going on between us." She turned to look at Hudson, noting the flush of embarrassment coloring his face as he avoided eye contact. "I'm just here because of Eli. If Hudson trusts you, I do too. I promise not to get in your way or cause any trouble.

I'll be out of here as soon as I can figure something else out."

"You're welcome in our home as long you as need," Angie said, waving a hand at her husband to prevent him from saying whatever he was about to.

"I appreciate that." She walked over and took Eli from Hudson, who didn't resist or even make eye contact. "All I care about is keeping this baby boy safe. And not getting killed in the meantime."

Angie and Logan looked at each other, then back at her and finally at Hudson. "How about some coffee and snacks while you two bring us up to speed? We're here for you—whatever you need. Hudson, you know that."

He nodded. "That's why I'm here. Thank you."

Angie returned to the kitchen, and soon the smell of freshly brewed goodness filled the house. Ava busied herself changing Eli's diaper and fixing him a bottle. Thankfully, she'd learned that skill over the years.

As if Angie had heard her thoughts, she appeared beside Ava, setting a cup of coffee on the end table beside her. "Your little boy is precious."

Ava looked up briefly. "Oh no, he's not mine. He's, um, kind of in protective custody at the moment."

Angie smiled as she rubbed the baby's hair gently.

"He looks so much like Hudson that I'd sort of hoped maybe he'd come to his senses and just forgot to mention it to us."

"Nope." Ava tried not to sound curt, but Angie's words had definitely struck a raw nerve.

"So, you and Hudson are here together because...?" Angie looked confused.

Ava bundled Eli back up in his blanket and settled into the sofa to give him a bottle. "We were sort of forced together because of little Elijah here."

"You named him?" Angie sat beside her, sipping from her own mug.

"No. There was a note when he was abandoned." She decided against telling Angie that Eli might belong to Quinn. Hudson could share whatever information he wanted to, but Ava wasn't going to be the one who opened that can of worms—particularly since she had no idea how he actually knew these people. They sure seemed to know plenty about her, though.

Ava turned her attention to Eli, who was drinking greedily. She picked up his tiny hand and rubbed the back of it with her thumb. "I guess you were hungry, little man. You never let on. I'm sorry I didn't know."

"You're a natural," Angie said. "I felt like a clumsy

idiot when our little Isabella was born. I had no idea how to do anything."

"It's my business. I place babies through private adoption." Ava set Eli's hand down on his chest and picked up the mug of coffee. It felt way too hot to have near him, so she set it down again.

"I didn't realize Sunrise had an adoption agency." Angie set her own cup down on the coffee table. "With such a tiny population, I guess I didn't expect there to be a need."

Ava shrugged. "We serve all of North Carolina and Southern Virginia. There's more need than most people realize."

She looked over at the kitchen to see Hudson and Logan huddled over some papers. He must have felt her gaze on him because he looked up and gave her a little nod. It kind of annoyed her that she had been left out of their discussion when it was her life in the balance.

Angie must have sensed her irritation. "You must be exhausted," she observed, diverting Ava's attention from the two men.

"What I want more than sleep is a shower. And maybe to wash these nasty clothes." Ava looked down at the clothes she'd borrowed from Hudson what seemed like ages ago.

"Of course! Once the baby is done eating, I'll show you and Hudson where you'll sleep. There's an en suite bathroom with everything you need. I'll grab you some of my clothes to wear too. You're a bit taller than me, but I'm rounder, so it should even out." Angie jumped up off the couch and soon disappeared.

Hudson and Logan fist-bumped. Logan picked up one of the papers that appeared to be a map and folded it. Hudson tucked a few others into his pocket. Ava kept trying not to get angry that the two of them had just obviously had a conversation that would directly affect her future without including her.

Angie returned and motioned for them to follow her. Ava carried Eli, and Logan grabbed the diaper bag. Letting Logan lead the way, followed by Hudson, Ava couldn't help but think about the long hot shower she would be taking in just a matter of minutes.

Angie led them into a large room. It had a queen bed, a sofa, and a baby bed all set up for sleeping. There were clothes laid out for her and Hudson on the bed.

"You have such an interesting home," Ava said, looking around and noting that there were no windows in the large room. "From the outside, I would never guess how big it is."

Angie gave her a smile. "Logan followed in his aunt Clara's footsteps in having the home built into the mountainside. It makes heating and cooling extremely easy, since we don't get electricity this far up."

"Then how are the lights on?" Ava asked, feeling foolish even saying the words.

"Solar power. We have a battery system that collects the energy and powers our entire property." Their hostess walked over to the baby bed. "I still had Isabella's playpen in the closet of her room, so I set it up for sweet Eli to sleep in. There are some extra blankets and things for him on top of the bureau." Gesturing through a door to the small den beyond and the sofa it housed, she said, "Hudson, you get the couch in there. Don't worry, Logan says it's comfy. He may have spent a night or two in here over the years." She winked at Ava, then stood on tiptoe and kissed Logan on the cheek. "Sometimes my man gets himself put in the doghouse."

Hudson clapped his friend on the shoulder. "Still making trouble even in your golden years, my man?"

Logan raised an eyebrow. "Dude, you're as old as I am."

Hudson shrugged. "What can I say? I age better than you."

Angie laughed as she took Logan by the hand and led him to the door. "Okay, you two, it's time to say goodnight."

"Yes, dear," Logan said, grinning as he let his wife lead him away.

After the door closed and they were alone, Hudson turned to Ava. "Would you like to shower first?"

She practically melted with gratitude. "Yes, please."

"Here." He reached for Eli. "Let me put him down. Take your time in there. I know how long this day has been."

She sighed as she handed the baby to Hudson. "How long the past few days have been."

Angie had left her a pair of black leggings, a sports bra, and a long-sleeved shirt that looked like they would fit perfectly. Grabbing the garments off the bed, Ava headed to the bathroom.

As soon as she closed the bathroom door, she collapsed against it, leaning into the cool wood. Seeing her reflection in the mirror over the sink, she gasped. She'd totally forgotten about the wound on her head. Her curls were a tangled rat's nest, and there was a dark smudge of dirt running along the length of her chin on the left side of her face.

"Good Lord, they must think I'm a real hot mess," she said, looking up toward the ceiling. "That's because I *am* a hot mess."

Turning on the water in the large walk-in shower, she studied herself in the mirror while it heated up. A decent-sized bruise had formed where she'd whacked her head on the dashboard that morning. Was it really only that morning? It felt like a lifetime ago. At least Ranger Bobby had fixed her up pretty well. The cut didn't look bad, although it would probably scar.

As steam filled the space, she stripped out of the dirty clothes she wore and stepped into the hot water. The steady stream felt amazing on her aching body. She stayed there a long time before reluctantly admitting that she needed to give Hudson a turn. After a quick toweling off, she dressed in the clothes Angie had lent to her and exited the bathroom with a comb in her hand that she'd found in a drawer.

HUDSON WAS SITTING ON THE SOFA IN THE little den, staring at the wall, completely absorbed in his thoughts. He never even heard Ava enter the room.

"I'm sorry I took so long. The hot water and soap just felt so good."

He turned to look at her and sucked in a breath. The way she was standing there with wet curls draped around her shoulders reminded him of their last trip to the beach and their first and only kiss. "Do you feel better?"

She smiled. "Definitely. How's Eli?"

"Sound asleep in the little bed thing." He waved in the direction of the bedroom. "Sit down for a minute? I want to fill you in on a few things before we call it a night."

He didn't want to tell her about the two men who had been after her, and he definitely didn't want her to know about his recon plan with Logan in the morning, but he felt she deserved some sort of explanation about who wanted her dead.

"Okay." Ava sat cross-legged on the other end of the sofa with her back against the arm of it so she could face him. "What's up?"

Hudson pulled some folded papers from his pocket and handed them to her. She opened them and studied the pictures, her expression changing from fear to worry to anger in a matter of seconds. She handed the papers back.

"These are the men who have been after me?" She narrowed her eyes and scrunched her nose in annoyance. "What could people like them want with someone like me? This can't be about any of the kids I've placed. It has to do with Eli."

He shifted so he also sat sideways on the couch and faced Ava. "My best guess based on everything is that Eli is the son of a cartel boss. I know it's way out there, and it might just be my detective's brain trying to make connections, but I don't know what else it could be. You, Eli, and the men are all connected somehow. Tomorrow, Logan and I are going to try to figure it all out."

"What?" Her eyes widened as she clapped a hand over her mouth. "A cartel boss? You can't actually be serious, here."

"I'm afraid so. That's what Logan and I were discussing. Being a local cop, he knows the crime element in the area pretty well. He told me there's a compound not far from here that is believed to house some pretty shady characters. When he checked the address, it matched the last-known address of Creep One and Creep Two." He waved the papers in the air. "And it explains *why* they have the same address. As far as Logan knows, there's another, smaller compound not far from Sunrise in the Outer Banks. It's an outpost with a small marina of its own. Deliveries are taken there, he thinks."

"Where does Quinn come into play in all of this?" Ava looked a little overwhelmed with all the information, but as long as she had questions, he'd try to answer them.

He exhaled, knowing she wouldn't like his response. "Honestly, I'm not sure she does." He was right. Her mouth opened to reply, but he held up a hand to stop her. "I'm also not sure she doesn't."

She looked so sad. He hated to be the one to have made her feel that way. But facts were facts, and evidence... well, they didn't have a whole lot of that at the moment. He could only go on what they *did* have, which wasn't much at all. He reached over and picked up her hand, squeezing it lightly in his. "You've been through so much the last couple days. I'm sorry any of it has happened."

Holding her hand felt like the most natural thing in the world, and he wanted to keep doing it, but Ava pulled it out of his grasp, a hint of confusion in her green eyes.

"I'm choosing to have faith."

He narrowed his eyes at her. "What does belief in

God have to do with this?"

"Call it fate. Or karma. Whatever you want. I'm choosing to believe that all this has happened for a reason. The baby, the note—even the guys who are after me."

"You believe it's all part of some grand plan to leave me without my family? That fate decided it was okay for my parents to die in a storm or for my sister to disappear? I refuse to accept that. I didn't want to be alone for the rest of my life."

As soon as those last words left his mouth, he knew he'd hurt her. Again. Apparently, he'd become a real pro at it.

"It didn't have to be that way, you know."

He didn't reply. Her words cut too deep.

"What happened to us, Hudson?" Ava asked, looking not at him but at the hand he'd just held. "We should have helped each other through Quinn's... disappearance, not pushed each other away."

She still referred to Quinn as missing, not dead the way he had for a decade. Maybe she deserved Quinn's love more than he ever had for not giving up on her. The way he'd given up on them. He certainly didn't deserve either of them at the moment.

"It just hurt too much, Ava. Looking at you every

day would have been a constant reminder of everything I'd lost."

She sighed. "Or of the love you'd gained. I never would have wanted to replace Quinn. I just wanted to be with you."

Her face turned red as her eyes grew moist, and Ava looked away.

"I... I just couldn't." Hudson exhaled heavily. "I wanted to be with you, but it just hurt so much. I miss my parents. And Quinn. Her death left me alone in the world, and I didn't know how to exist that way. Getting married without any of them around... it would have just been too much."

She swiped at a few stray tears. "That's the thing. You *weren't* alone. You had me."

"We were just so young. *I* was too young. I had no idea how to deal with what had happened. And then I was angry." He looked away. "Angry at God. Angry at the world. And angry at you. It was easier to just box it all up and put it away. Start fresh, I guess. I joined the police department, bought my house, and threw everything I had into those two things."

"Did you?"

Her question confused him. "Did I what?"

She rolled her eyes at him, the way she used to when they were teenagers and wanted him to know he was clueless. "*Did* you start over? Or did you just live in the shadow of what you'd lost without actually moving forward?"

Oh boy, did her question strike a nerve. He stood up and walked over to the small stone fireplace across the room, trying to buy time to figure out how to answer Ava. Because she really had hit something deep inside that stung. She sat still on the sofa, watching him with those emerald-green eyes he'd committed to memory so long ago.

"I tried. Was I successful? In some ways. I have a great career." He gave a small smile. "And you saw my yard."

She laughed a little. "Your yard is amazing. But I don't think you've moved forward. I think you just fixed yourself up with the life you thought you deserved. It's been ten years, Hudson. Shouldn't you have considered a family of your own at some point? Let go of the sadness and seek some happiness?"

He narrowed his eyes at her. "Is that what you did? Or did you find a career that made you feel like you were righting a huge wrong, a little bit at a time?"

Ava jumped up from the sofa, her expression angry and looking for a battle. "Isn't that what *you* did?"

Had he done that with police work? Again, she tweaked an already raw nerve.

"No." At least he didn't think so. "I'm good at police work."

She stuck her hands on her hips. "And I am great at adoption placements. My career serves people. That's what I always wanted out of life. I had just hoped to do it with you in my life."

"I'm sorry, Ava. I just couldn't—it was too hard."

They stood there, eyeing each other for a full sixty seconds, waiting to see who would crack first. Finally she exhaled. "Hudson, there's something I think you should know."

The look in her eyes scared him a little. Whatever she wanted to say, it wasn't going to be good. "What is it?"

As she opened her mouth to reply, Eli let out a shrill cry.

Ava rushed from the room and picked the baby up. Listening to her coo and whisper to him had his heart doing all sorts of crazy things. She would make an amazing mother someday. Whatever man won her heart over would be the luckiest man alive. He'd already ruined any chances he had of a future and a life with her, but he certainly wished all of those things for her.

Hudson headed to the bathroom to shower. He pulled off his clothes and stepped under the hot spray, letting the water wash away the day as much as it could. Ava's expression had him worried. Whatever she'd been about to say, he felt certain it would have changed everything.

Once he'd dried off, he slipped into the T-shirt and jogging pants Angie had left him. As tall as Hudson was, Logan had him by a couple inches, so the pants pooled at his ankles. It didn't really matter either way at the moment; he just knew he needed sleep and time for his brain to process all that had just been said. Truth be told, he'd never been as grateful for a crying baby as he had been in that moment. A lot of harsh realities had presented themselves, and he didn't know if he could have mentally handled whatever it was Ava had been about to say.

He wondered if he'd made some huge mistakes in the aftermath of Quinn's disappearance. How could Ava still be so strong in her convictions? She'd lost her best friend and the man who'd been telling her he loved her at the very same moment Quinn had disappeared, yet she'd moved forward in life. She was well respected in the community and loved by everyone.

Settling in on the sofa and pulling a blanket up over himself, Hudson attempted to push the image of

Ava and Eli from his mind and focus on trying to fall asleep. The visual of her holding the baby played on repeat, though, and was a reminder of how much he'd really given up when he pushed her away. He sighed, frustration filling him. If he didn't get some rest, the next couple days would be really exhausting. Recon day would be there in just a few short hours, and he had a feeling it would be rough.

NINE

Ava lay awake for a long time after Eli finally settled down. Poor little guy no doubt missed his mother something fierce. She felt helpless, knowing there was nothing she could do to fix that. Not yet anyway.

The discussion she'd been having with Hudson prior to Eli waking had all her emotions tied in knots and her mind racing. She'd always known he intentionally pushed her away after Quinn disappeared, but she didn't realize how deep-seated his anger and blame toward her went. Even if he'd warmed up some the last few days, it was his naturally protective nature that had him doing so. It had become blatantly obvious to her that he would push her away harder and faster than he had last time when this whole mess was over and done with.

The fact that she'd been about to tell him Quinn's secret—the one she'd sworn to take to the grave with her—added to her turmoil. Not because she'd been about to break that promise but because she hadn't done it a long time ago.

She'd do it in the morning.

By the time she finally drifted off to sleep, Ava had replayed the entire conversation on repeat in her brain at least half a dozen times. Then she'd gone back over ten years of occasional encounters with Hudson at the cemetery and finally back to the day Quinn disappeared.

Exhaustion eventually claimed her, although she woke up still trying to work through everything she felt.

Did she still love Hudson?

Sometimes it felt like she'd never stopped. At other times, she could swear they'd never met, and her infatuation had been at a distance.

Knowing he'd been angry at her for "distracting" him, which made him feel they were both responsible for what happened to Quinn, added a new twist to the emotional roller coaster she now rode. Once he knew what she knew, that roller coaster would be impossible to navigate.

Eli stirred and let out a little cry. Ava got up and lifted him out of the playpen. "Hey, little man. I bet you're hungry and need a diaper change."

Grabbing the diaper bag, she then set it on the bed and laid Eli down. After tackling the wet diaper, she put some formula powder in a bottle. His cries got progressively louder, letting her know his hunger had become more intense.

Hudson appeared in the doorway between the rooms. "Need some help?"

She nodded and held out the bottle. "Can you add some warm water to that?"

He frowned, the little furrow between his eyes deepening. "I don't think you're supposed to use tap water."

"It's all we have right now. I'm sure it will be fine." She picked up Eli, patting his back lightly to try and calm him. In the battle between a hungry baby and tap water, the hungry baby was determined to win.

Hudson disappeared into the bathroom and returned with a full bottle. "Here you go, little man." Handing it to Ava, he then led her to the sofa in the small attached room.

The tension surrounding them put her on edge.

Their conversation the night before had obviously affected him as well. They probably needed to revisit the topic at some point and try to reach a place they could both live with—at least while they were forced to be together.

He stood in front of her, looking incredibly uncomfortable. Pretending not to notice he was even there, she talked softly to Eli while he ate.

"Ava?" Hudson sounded as uncomfortable as he had looked.

She glanced up, trying to maintain a neutral expression. "Yes?"

He shifted his weight, looking every bit like a sixteen-year-old trying to squeak out a prom invitation. "About our talk last night."

Ava waved a hand in the air, dismissing the comment. "There's nothing left to discuss." Oh yes there was, but she wasn't ready to do it right then. Eventually, yes. But not at that moment. It would do Hudson some good to be left wondering, the way she had been for so long.

AVA'S SHUTDOWN CAUGHT HIM OFF GUARD. He'd expected to pick up where they'd left off in rehashing the past. He'd lain awake half the night, replaying not only their discussion but the last ten years and the day Quinn vanished. He'd never wanted to admit that it was possible he'd wrongly assumed his sister had died for so long. Convincing himself she'd died, even without a body, was far easier than accepting any other likelihood. Kidnapping and human trafficking had always been a possibility, he supposed. The other option, the one he'd never entertained but had occurred to him around two in the morning, hurt too much to think about.

Had his little sister intentionally disappeared, leaving him and Ava to grieve and hurt for a decade?

As soon as the thought presented itself, he'd dismissed it. Human trafficking was far less painful to consider, because then it would be someone else's fault she'd disappeared.

These were all the things he wanted to discuss with Ava. But she'd shut him down, and he had no idea how to approach the subject again.

"Hudson?"

He looked over at Ava, who wore a questioning look. "Everything okay with Eli?"

She nodded. "Yes. I was wrong. There's still something we need to discuss."

The seriousness of her tone worried him. The

look in her eyes cut him through the heart. Whatever she had to say, he knew it would hurt. "What is it?"

Ava sighed, looking like she carried the weight of the world on her shoulders. "It's something I should have told you a long time ago."

All his fears and middle-of-the-night worries wrapped around him and squeezed while he waited for her to continue.

"It's a promise I made to Quinn. Before she... disappeared. Until the last couple days, I never thought it had anything to do with what happened, or I swear I would have told you before."

If he didn't know better, he'd think she was afraid of him. Her green eyes had lost their luster and were growing dark with worry.

He dropped onto his knees in front of her, his eyes searching hers. "You can tell me anything, Ava. You know that, right?"

Eli grunted at the disruption to his food. Ava took a deep breath. "Quinn had a boyfriend."

Hudson chuckled. "Quinn had a lot of boyfriends."

She shook her head. "This one was different, Hudson. She was in love. But he was older than she was, and she knew you'd never approve."

He jumped to his feet and started pacing. "My

sister had a secret boyfriend? Impossible! Quinn and I always talked about everything."

Tears ran down both of Ava's cheeks now. "I'm so sorry, Hudson, but she did. He was older, and she really loved him. I met him once. His name was Ricky. I never heard his last name."

He stopped moving and stared down at her. "You met him? And never told me?"

She shrugged. "She made me swear to keep it a secret. After a while she stopped talking about him, so I figured she'd broken up with him."

Anger flooded his body. "And when she disappeared, you didn't think to mention this secret relationship?"

"The police said she'd drowned. The rip currents were awful that day, and you accepted that she'd died. Why would I dredge up the past and add to your sadness? You really didn't need to know that Quinn kept such a major secret from you."

He frowned so hard his head ached. "So you thought I needed this information now? Why, Ava?"

She looked up at him through her tears, but her voice remained steady. "When you showed me the photos of those guys, one of them looked familiar. I think he was there when I met Quinn's boyfriend. I can't be sure, since it was so long ago, but something in his eyes... something icy cold sent a chill through me back then, and it happened again when I saw the picture."

Hudson dropped onto the sofa beside her. "Do you know what this means?"

She nodded. "That maybe Quinn is actually alive?"

He exhaled heavily, feeling completely deflated and defeated. "That my sister has been out there somewhere for a *decade*, and I never looked for her. She might be held against her will—or worse—and I've done nothing."

Hudson leaned forward, resting his head in his hands.

Ava placed a hand on his back. "I think I'm going to go with you and Logan today."

Her words brought forth a flurry of fear that presented itself as anger. "Absolutely not."

Her features quickly morphed into anger of her own. "Yeah? Why not? You're just checking things out, right?"

"You need to stay with Eli."

She set the empty bottle down, shifted the baby to her shoulder, and patted his back gently. "I'm going to ask Angie to keep him for a bit while we go."

Her nonchalance made him crazy. "This is no

Sunday drive by the beach. You don't know what we'll see or what will happen."

She shrugged. "Neither do you. I'm as much a part of this as you are." Ava pointed at the baby. "Besides, I owe it to Quinn to try and help you find her."

Frustration made his pulse pound. The very thought of Ava anywhere near those men who had been trying to get to her set his entire body on edge. "You do realize we are going to be looking for some very bad guys. Men who have actually tried to kill you?"

"Yes, of course." Eli let out a loud burp. Ava laughed, and Hudson frowned.

"This is not a game, Ava."

She set Eli on the couch beside her, wrapped him in his blanket, and then stood up, holding him close. "I'm going to find Angie and ask her to look after Eli for a bit. Once we finish the mission, I'd like to stop at a store and get some more supplies for him and maybe a few things for myself."

It took all his self-control not to blow up. Then a separate round of frustration moved in over the fact that he felt so protective of Ava when all he should be focused on now was maybe finding his sister. Telling himself he only wanted to keep her safe because it was the right thing to do and had nothing to do with his feelings toward her from the past that he had begun to revisit, he changed tactics. "Ava. Please. Think about this."

"I did. And it's something I need to do."

Now he was confused. "Why?"

"You made me realize last night that I might be partly responsible for Quinn's disappearance, and now I want to right whatever wrong I may have caused."

He frowned. "That's ridiculous. You had no control over what happened then or whatever is happening now."

Ava raised an eyebrow in question. "You're confusing the heck out of me, Hudson. First you say you've been angry at me for a *decade*, blaming me for your sister being gone, and now you say it's ridiculous for me to think I had something to do with it? Even after what I just told you? Make up your mind already!"

She had him there. Everything he'd thought to be true for so long seemed to all be a lie. Now he had to accept the fact that he'd pushed away the one person he ever really loved instead of embracing her and navigating their grief together.

He pounded a fist against his thigh in frustration, exhaling through the pain. "Fine. You can go. If

Angie agrees to keep Eli. He has to be safe, above all else."

Ava nodded, almost cracking a tiny smile. He could see her lip twitch in one corner. "I agree. I'm going to find Angie. I'll be ready to leave whenever you and Logan are."

She'd won, and she knew it. He'd never been able to say no to her. Maybe that was part of the reason he'd pushed her away; she would have easily convinced him that Quinn's death—or disappearance as it may actually have been—wasn't his fault. And he really needed to believe it was.

Hudson took a quick shower, dressed in some more borrowed clothes, and was in the middle of combing his hair when a knock at the door interrupted him.

"Come in!" He set the comb on the bathroom counter and headed out to the main room just as Logan walked through the door. "Hey, buddy. Thanks again for taking us in with no warning. I had no place else to take them that would be safe."

Logan nodded. "It's nice to see someone using Aunt Clara's rooms. It's been a while since she visited, and as you can see, there's plenty of space."

"How is your aunt?" Hudson tucked his wallet and

cell phone into his pockets and clipped his badge to his belt.

"You know, planning for the end of the world as always. She married one of her prepper friends, and her place on the mountain is a regular compound." Logan stepped back toward the door. "You ready to head out?"

Hudson exhaled. "Yeah. There's been a change of plans, though."

Logan chuckled. "I know. Ava is going with us. Angie and Bella are busy fawning over Eli as we speak. Ava is pacing the hall by the door, waiting."

"You don't think it's a bad idea to let her go?" Hudson asked as he followed Logan out of the room.

"Not at all. She's as much a part of this as you are, *and* she's pretty dang smart. I'd want her on my team if she were a cop."

"You got all that from last night?" They entered the living room. Hudson could hear Angie and her daughter talking and giggling in the kitchen.

"I'm a detective, just like you. It's my job to read people." Logan leaned into the kitchen and blew his wife a kiss. Angie ran over and gave him a big smack on the lips. A tiny pang of jealousy struck Hudson somewhere around his heart, but he pushed it aside. Like every emotion other than anger he'd felt during the last ten years, he pretended it didn't exist.

They found Ava pacing the hall, just as Logan had said. "What took you two so long?"

Hudson punched Logan lightly on the arm. "Lover boy had to get smoochy with his wife."

Embarrassment colored Logan's face. "She gave me one kiss goodbye! It's tradition. Just wait until you get married. Then you'll understand."

Hudson glanced over at Ava, who seemed to be making a point of *not* looking at him.

"You two ready?" she asked.

"Let's do this," Logan replied.

They took Logan's Jeep, since the shooters had never seen it. Ava sat quietly in the back. Her silence worried him. She didn't utter a single word during the entire forty-five-minute ride.

"See that stone wall right there?" Logan pointed at an eight-foot structure in front of them. "That's the edge of the cartel property. Surrounds it all the way around."

Hudson didn't like the looks of that wall. Security was going to be tough. "Do you know which cartel we're dealing with?"

Logan pulled his Jeep to the side of the road and put it in Park. "The Baron cartel. They move guns and dabble in drugs but prefer the trade of human trafficking."

"Human trafficking?" Ava exclaimed. "You mean Quinn might be...?"

Hudson turned to look at her over the seat. He felt her obvious anguish go straight to the center of his soul. "No one is saying that. If Eli belongs to Quinn, then she's not been sold or anything like that."

"Um, Hud?" Logan said. "I wouldn't necessarily say that. She could be a local sale."

His friend's words struck an uneasy chord in him. One he'd been trying very hard to ignore. "Don't even say that," he ground out between clenched teeth.

Logan frowned but didn't say any more about it. "I think we should get out and look around on foot. The Jeep might call attention to us."

"Sounds like a plan. Ava, you'll stay with me," Hudson said.

She folded her arms over her chest. "I'm a big girl. I can go alone."

He turned in his seat so they could see each other. "But I have a gun, and you don't. I guarantee everyone behind that wall has one too."

He could tell she wanted to dig her heels in, but she finally relented. "Fine. Unless one of you has an extra gun you'd want to share with me? Then no one would be stuck with me."

Logan chuckled. "I like her, Hud."

They exited the Jeep and headed off in two different directions.

"I could have gone with your friend, you know," Ava said as they climbed a small incline at the base of the wall.

The thought of her spending time with Logan made him a bit jealous. "It's my job to keep you safe. You know, for Eli and the case." He had absolutely no intention of letting her get hurt. Or worse. He definitely wasn't sending her off alone with Logan, no matter how good of friends they were.

"The case, right." She sounded a little disappointed. Or maybe it was just what he wanted to hear. Either way, they had a job to accomplish at the moment. He could examine some of the things that had been bugging him since the night before. Their conversation that morning had really been weighing on him as well. The thought that his sister, the person he'd been closest to in the world, had kept such a major secret from him hurt far more than he wanted to admit.

They walked along the length of the wall in silence until they hit one of the corners. Nearby there stood a large tree with excellent climbing potential. If he could shimmy up there and get a look over the wall—

"What exactly are we looking for?" Ava asked, sounding a bit impatient.

"That." He pointed at the tree.

She looked at him, confused. "A tree?"

"It's got plenty of branches and goes high enough that I can see over the wall." He strode toward it, already planning his path upward.

"Oh." Ava followed him but didn't say anything else as he pulled himself up into the first crook of the trunk and began his ascent.

His foot slipped, but he caught himself before he fell.

"Maybe I should be the one to climb the tree? Twelve years of gymnastics training, remember?" she said, sounding worried.

"I've got it, thanks." From somewhere in the distance, he heard a dog bark and a man yell.

"I sure hope that wasn't Logan," he murmured as he continued to climb.

He set his foot on a branch that cracked when he put pressure on it. Skipping that one, he climbed to the next. Ava stood below, looking down at something on her cell phone.

When he reached the perfect vantage point, he looked back down to signal her. She was gone.

"Ava!" he whisper-shouted as loud as he dared. "Ava! Where are you?"

"MEN ALWAYS WANT TO DO THINGS THE HARD way." Ava looked back at the map on her phone. The rise she sought should be coming up very soon.

Another hundred feet or so and she reached her destination—a vantage point high enough for her to see over the wall without climbing trees.

She scanned the area, settling her focus on a large stone patio. As she watched, one of the several screened doors opened, and a woman stepped out, followed closely by an older man. The man had his hand resting on the woman's lower back as he directed her toward two chairs.

The woman stepped away from him and walked over to a lounge chair, away from the ones the man had selected. Something familiar in the way she moved caught Ava's attention.

Opening the camera app on her cell phone, she aimed it at the patio and zoomed in just as the woman turned in her direction.

Ava gasped, dropping her phone.

She scooped it up and refocused the camera. Had she actually just seen what she thought she had?

Catching the woman in her screen again, Ava sucked in a breath. She was older, definitely, but there was absolutely no doubt in her mind that the woman she stared at was Quinn.

Her heart rate kicked up several notches as Quinn glanced in her direction. Hidden in the brush and trees, Ava knew Quinn couldn't actually see her. Still, she could barely contain herself from calling out. What she needed to do was get back to Hudson. Hopefully, he'd seen her, too, from his perch in the tree.

Voices carried over the wall, diverting her attention for a moment. She could see two—no, three men moving around the well-manicured lawn in front of the Spanish-style mansion covered in a light-colored stucco. Ava moved along the wall, attempting to get a good look at them. It could help to know what they were up against when they rescued Quinn. Unfortunately, the terracotta roof with the copper flashing caught the sunlight and directed it straight at her, making it nearly impossible to see what the men actually looked like. The best she could make out was that they were all of similar build and well strapped with guns and ammunition. More than likely they acted as security for the compound, and they definitely took their job seriously.

She snapped a few pictures of them to show Hudson and Logan later.

Returning to her vantage point, she zoomed in on her long-lost friend again. Quinn's blue eyes that once danced with mischief all the time seemed to have gone dull. Of course, Ava was looking through a phone camera, so it could have been her imagination, but she didn't think so.

The man with her resembled the secret boyfriend Ava had met so long ago, but she didn't think he was the man named Ricky. If he was, he'd aged ridiculously in a decade. They appeared to be arguing. Quinn had always been very passionate when she believed in something. Whatever they were discussing, she seemed to be confident that she was the one who was right.

Snapping several pictures of Quinn, the man with her, and the patio area, Ava watched until her friend rose from the chair and went into the house.

She had to tell Hudson. Right away.

She ran back to the tree where she'd left him, bursting at the seams with joy and excitement that Quinn was alive!

GLANCING AROUND BELOW ONCE MORE, hoping to see Ava, Hudson shifted his position for a better view. This let him see that there were two armed men heading in his direction, but Ava still remained out of sight.

A fierce growl below him forced his attention in that direction.

"What the—"

A black Doberman, teeth bared, stared up at him. He growled again as he rose onto his hind legs and scratched at the tree trunk.

"Nice doggy. I'm not going to hurt you." Like he could do anything perched in a tree like a darned bird. Looking around for something to toss, he saw a broken branch stuck in the solid ones a few feet away. Stretching as much as possible, his fingers brushed it, but he couldn't grab hold.

The dog jumped and swiped at him, barely missing one of his feet. The growling continued, saliva dripping from the animal's jowls.

"Good puppy. You want a stick to play with? Here, let me find you a good stick." Hudson reached again for the broken branch and made contact. Unfortunately, his sudden movement knocked it loose, sending the stick to the ground.

"Damn it!"

The dog jumped again, a little higher this time, and caught the hem of his jeans with a sharp claw. As the dog fell back to the ground, it had enough purchase to yank Hudson with it. Hudson fell backward and hung upside down from the branch by his knees. With his hands dangling and his head three feet closer to the angry mutt below, he finally started to panic.

The dog barked, intermittently taking time to growl and swipe at him. Hudson did his best to swing out of the way, but a couple times, those giant paws with the sharp nails came way too close to his head for comfort.

He frantically searched for some way to pull himself up. Loud voices calling and whistling for the dog added to his panic.

"Brutal! Where are you, boy?" a man's voice yelled. "Brutal! Whatcha got, boy?"

As Brutal made one last swipe for him, dragging a sharp nail across Hudson's cheek, someone came crashing through the trees on the outside of the wall. Prepared to be discovered, he tried one more time to right himself and finally managed to get a grip on a branch.

Something heavy smashed into Brutal. The dog let out a sharp yelp, then took off toward the man calling for him, whimpering and limping.

"Thank you," he whispered as he swung from the branch and dropped down to the ground below. As he stumbled backward and landed on his backside, blood ran into the corner of his mouth. Swiping at the dog scratch, he discovered that the wound was pretty deep.

"Hudson!" Ava grabbed his hand and yanked at him. "Come on! We have to get out of here! The men will find us!"

Scrambling to his feet, he let her hold his hand as she led him away. "Ava! Where have you been?"

"Later! Come on. We need to hide." She tugged harder. "This way!"

After a few seconds, they encountered a lake. She ran to the edge and jumped into a rowboat that looked older than he was.

"*Hudson!* Get in!"

He did as he was told, then pushed the rickety structure away from the shore.

Ava rowed with a fierceness he hadn't seen from her before. When he tried to take the oars, she pushed him away. "You're hurt. I've got this. We just need to get around that bend over there. The dog will lose our trail in the water."

The adrenaline that had spiked when the dog came after him had begun to recede. Hudson sat back against the wall of the boat to ride out the crash. His face hurt like the dickens, and his heart still pounded in his chest.

TEN

THE MEN'S SHOUTS AND THE DOG'S BARKS grew louder as they got closer to the lake. Ava rowed for all she was worth, finally getting the small boat into a treed area on the opposite shore. The land had formed a small cove that provided natural protection from sight. She set the oars down, then jumped out and pulled the little boat onto the shore.

"Come on, Hudson. We have to go."

He opened his eyes and looked around, obviously confused. "Did I pass out?"

She shrugged. "I'm not sure. We need to get into the trees, though. Can you walk?"

He nodded. "Yeah, I'm pretty sure I can." He accepted her hand again and let her lead him deep into the trees.

When Ava saw Hudson hanging from that tree with a nasty gash on his face and that dog attacking him, her heart had dropped straight into her stomach. All she could think about was saving him and getting out of there. Her excitement at her own discovery had quickly been replaced with panic as she searched for something to save him. Her annoyance at him went up in smoke as she tossed the heavy rock at the mutt, hitting its back end and sending it off to wherever it had come from.

"We need to call Logan. He's going to worry," Hudson said when they finally stopped walking.

"Go ahead. Text him. I think we're far enough in to be safe."

She waited while he sent the text, straining to hear any sounds that didn't belong in the woods. The voices and barking had faded away. Hopefully, their pursuers had given up.

When Hudson finished his text, he put his phone in his pocket. "Logan said okay. He'll meet us at the Jeep as soon as we can get there."

Ava nodded and pointed to the trees. "There should be a path through there that will take us around the lake. It'll probably spit us out not far from the Jeep."

He furrowed his brow as he narrowed his eyes at her. "How do you know that?"

She held up her phone. "Google Earth. While you were playing Tarzan climbing that tree, I pulled up the view of the area and checked it out."

Hudson grasped her upper arms suddenly. "Thank you for saving me." With one hand, he tilted her chin up to make her look at him. "I mean it, Ava. I was about to become dog kibble."

She reached up and touched the spot on his cheek above the dog scratch. "You scared me half to death, Hudson. Seeing you hanging there like that with a crazy dog trying to drag you from the tree. I just couldn't—"

He nodded. "I know. Just... thank you."

As the adrenaline wore off, Ava suddenly needed to sit down. Quickly. Hudson must have sensed it, since he leaned down and scooped her up in his arms. Striding across the small clearing they were in, he then set her down on a short rock ledge. As he went to release her, she wrapped her arms around his torso and rested her head against his chest.

"Don't ever scare me like that again, do you understand? I just kept praying I could get that dog away from you." She squeezed her eyes closed to hold back the tears that threatened to escape.

Hudson ran a hand softly down her hair and pressed a kiss to the top of her head. "I'm fine, thanks to you. Why did you disappear? When I looked down and saw you were gone.... Where did you go?"

She pulled back from their embrace. "Remember I looked at Google Earth? I saw a rise in the land about halfway down the wall. I figured I could get a different view of the compound than you, and we could compare notes."

"But you didn't tell me. You just left." There was genuine worry in his features that made her feel a little warm and fuzzy.

Placing a palm against his uninjured cheek, she looked up at him and smiled, suddenly filled with all kinds of excitement again. "I'm sorry. I didn't mean to worry you. I just wanted to do my part. And guess what?"

"Um, what?"

"I saw her! I saw Quinn! She's alive!"

"Are you serious?" He looked as shocked as she had felt when she first saw Quinn walking out on the large stone patio, an older man close behind.

She nodded, barely able to contain her emotions. "She's hardly changed at all! At least from what I could see from so far away."

"I can't believe it. After all these years.... And you

never gave up hope, Ava." Hudson's eyes overflowed with tears as he crushed her in a hug, then planted a kiss on her lips.

As he pulled away from the kiss, they both froze, locked in a mutual stare that held many more questions than answers.

He suddenly jumped back as though she'd scalded him. "I'm so sorry, Ava. I don't know why I did that."

She had no idea how to respond. One part of her wanted to be mad at Hudson and tell him that whatever they'd had was gone for good. Another, louder part was jumping up and down, clapping hands, and shouting, *Do it again*! He was the only man she'd ever loved, and that had been ten years ago. It wasn't that she didn't go out on dates with other guys; it was just that none of them had interested her enough to have a second date, let alone do anything else. When Hudson kissed her, flames ignited and fireworks went off—then and now.

Touching her lips with her fingertips, she searched his eyes for some hint at how he felt about what had just happened. As always, he let nothing show.

"No need to apologize," she replied, more than a little saddened by his lack of emotion. "We were both excited, and old habits die hard, I suppose." Not that kissing Hudson had ever been or could ever become habitual. Ten years ago, every touch, no matter how insignificant, had been new and exciting. Holding hands, a kiss on the cheek—she used to treasure it all.

"I didn't—I mean, yeah, you're probably right. We just got caught up in the amazing news that Quinn might still be alive."

She pushed him away a little. "What do you mean, *might be*? I told you I saw her." She pulled out her phone and opened the camera app, shoving it at him. "*Look!*"

Hudson took her phone and studied the photo. He stared at it for so long, she got a little nervous. Maybe she'd been wrong after all. Finally, he reached up and lightly touched the screen. "You're right. She's hardly changed at all. Except for how sad she looks. Ava, we need to get her out of there."

"Why do you look so worried?"

He sighed, seemingly letting go of the weight of the world. "That man with Quinn is Rosario Baron. Head of the Baron cartel and one of the top persons of interest in human trafficking in this area. No one has ever been able to prove his connection to the trade, though. He has others do all his dirty work."

"I thought she looked sad, too, but she's not

scared. Maybe he isn't actually involved in anything that awful. Or maybe that's why she thought Eli wasn't safe?"

Hudson handed her back the phone. "Um, maybe because he's the son of a cartel leader?"

Realization slammed into her with the force of a tsunami. "That man isn't the one I met."

He shrugged. "He's got his hand at the small of her back. That's a pretty intimate touch for, say, a boss or a business colleague."

Ava frowned. "You don't think she...?"

"What?" he asked, looking worried.

"Well, that's not Ricky. What if she's been held hostage all this time? Part of the human trafficking thing Logan talked about?"

Hudson shook his head slowly, considering her question. "I really hope not, but I suppose anything is possible now."

Panic seized her. "We need to go find Logan and start planning how to get her out of there."

He reached up to grip her by the hips and lift her down from the rocks. His touch reignited the flames and fireworks his kiss had caused. His eyes darkened a little as he set her on her feet. Ava was shocked when he reached up and pressed a palm to her cheek. "Thank you."

She narrowed her eyes at him. "For what?"

"For always believing. For never giving up hope. And, finally, for making this stubborn man listen to you. I know it wasn't easy."

Ava smiled up at him, rose on tiptoe, and pressed a kiss to his chin—the only thing she could reach. "No, it wasn't. But I'm stubborn too. Which is maybe why the last decade went the way it did." She stepped around him and headed for the little trail she'd seen on Google Earth.

HUDSON WATCHED AS AVA WALKED AWAY FROM him while he considered the last few minutes. Her faith that Quinn was still alive had sustained her for all those years and had been proven true. She had the pictures to prove it. It made him seriously question almost every decision he'd made since that day, particularly the one where he'd chosen to believe his sister was dead rather than maintain hope. Pushing Ava away had also been proven a paramount mistake of epic proportions. He knew he'd messed up— royally. What he didn't know was how to start repairing the damage those mistakes had caused.

If he even could.

Ten years felt like a lifetime as he followed Ava down the narrow hunting path she'd located. He had a lot of time to make up for. For now, he'd focus on saving his sister. That had to be the priority. Afterward, he'd try to make it up to Ava for his lousy behavior however she'd let him.

"You're questioning your lack of faith right now, aren't you?" Ava had stopped walking and now stood looking at him with a curious expression.

"What makes you think that?"

She shrugged. "Because I would be if I were you. You spent a decade blaming me and probably Quinn for her disappearance. You pushed everyone away and let anger rule your life."

"How do you do it, Ava?" He kicked at a small rock in front of him. "You lost things, too, and yet you just go on with life like it never happened."

"First off, I do not. I've felt Quinn's loss—and yours—every single day. But I couldn't let myself wallow in self-pity. Instead, I took my sadness and channeled that energy into something that did some good in the world."

Running his fingers through his hair, Hudson sighed. "I'm sorry, Ava. I just didn't know how much you were hurting too."

"You never asked." She turned away and started

walking again. "I think we need to keep moving. Every moment we spend here takes time away from figuring out how to get Quinn out of that prison she's in."

They walked the rest of the way in near silence aside from an occasional "Watch out for that branch" or "Be careful of that hole in the path." He had a lot to think about, but it would all have to wait. Quinn's rescue had become his top priority now. Ava's use of Google Earth could be very helpful to him in figuring out how to make that happen. Hopefully, Logan had gathered some useful information as well.

A full hour's hike later, they emerged onto the main road. Logan's Jeep reflected the afternoon sun as they made their way toward it.

Once they arrived, Logan stepped out of the driver's seat. "I was getting worried. Man, you two look rough. Hudson! Buddy, what happened to your face?"

"A hungry mutt named Brutal."

Not in the mood to explain further, Hudson walked past his friend and got into the back seat of the Jeep. Logan and Ava climbed in the front, and they headed back home.

Angie and Bella were outside with Eli when they pulled up in front of the house. As soon as she saw

Hudson's face, Angie handed Eli to Ava and ran inside to lay out first aid supplies. Logan and Bella followed.

Ava hugged a smiling Eli close. Seeing them together, how much they already cared for each other, told Hudson all he needed to know about the family he could have had. Grunting, he walked past them and into the house also.

He heard Ava chatting with Eli as he left them outside. "It's okay, kiddo. Uncle Hudson is just a little cranky today. He really does love you."

"I am not cranky," he muttered as the door slammed closed behind him. "Okay, maybe just a little. But I'm entitled after the day I've had."

"Come into the kitchen, Hudson!" Angie called. "I'll help you clean that mess up. Might need stitches, you know."

"It's just a scratch," he replied, entering the kitchen. "I just need to wash it and put some antibacterial stuff on it."

Ava joined them just as Hudson patted the newly washed wound dry with a clean cloth. "Did he tell you?" she asked Angie.

Angie looked confused. "Tell me what?"

"She's alive! I saw Quinn. I have pictures. I was right all along." Ava danced in a circle around the kitchen with a laughing Eli in her arms. She kissed him on the forehead. "Your mama is coming home!"

"We still need to get her out of there. It looks like she might be romantically involved with Rosario Baron." Hudson winced as Angie dabbed the wound with some hydrogen peroxide.

"Who is Rosario Baron?" Angie asked, tossing the used gauze in the trash and then washing her hands.

"One of the world's most *suspected* human traffickers," Logan replied as he stepped into the kitchen from what looked like a closet. Since he was carrying a package of cookies, Hudson assumed it was actually a pantry.

His stomach growled loudly at the sight of the snack.

"Whoa, man, when did you eat last?" Logan shoved a cookie in his mouth, letting crumbs accumulate on the front of his shirt.

"Yesterday, I guess. I never stopped to grab anything before we left this morning."

Ava settled Eli on her hip. "Hang out a minute, and I'll make us some sandwiches. If Angie doesn't mind?"

"Not one bit! It'll be nice to be waited on in my own home for a change." She shot Logan a pointed look. "Why don't you let me take the little guy into the playroom and let Bella entertain him some while you do that?"

"Sounds great. I could see outside how good she is with him." Ava handed the baby to Angie, and she left the room with Logan in tow.

Hudson stepped over to the door Logan had come out of and pulled it open. The bright lights, full shelves, and staircase in the center of the floor were not at all what he had expected to find.

"What is that? Some kind of storm cellar?" Ava asked from behind him.

"I'm not 100 percent sure, but if my friend is anything like the woman who raised him, it's going to be absolutely amazing."

"I don't understand." She had stepped in beside him, still looking at all the shelves loaded down with jars of dried goods like beans, flour, sugar, and who knew what else.

"The best explanation is to just see it." Hudson started down the steps with Ava right behind him.

Halfway down, he flipped a switch, flooding the basement in bright light. Shelves lined three of the walls. They were filled with jars of home-canned fruits, vegetables, meats, soups, stews, and a dozen other things. The fourth wall had a different kind of storage system that housed paper goods, store-bought canned goods, and other random bits.

"Whoa!" Ava stood on the step behind him just high enough to let the breath she'd exhaled tickle the back of his neck.

"I know. Amazing, isn't it? His twin cousins and his aunt are the same way. No matter what happens in the world, they'll be fine and will probably outlive everyone else."

She walked past him and over to one of the walls to pick up a jar. "This one is labeled 'onion soup.' I wonder if it's any good."

His mouth watered, and his stomach growled again even louder than before. He laughed. "I sure hope so. My starving inner beast is about to crack open the lid and drink it from the jar."

Ava rubbed her abdomen lightly. "I know what you mean. I'm absolutely famished."

She headed to the staircase at the exact same time he did. When they collided, she stumbled. Hudson wrapped his arms around her to steady her.

"Thank you! I'd hate to waste this jar of soup with my clumsiness." Ava looked up at him. He liked the little flush filling her face and the slight uptick in her breathing as he held her.

"We definitely wouldn't want to lose that jar." He

reached up and smoothed some stray hairs back from her face, tucking them behind her ear.

She opened her mouth slightly as though she had something to say but changed her mind at the last second. His own heart rate kicked up a notch, matching hers. He knew it did because he felt her heart pounding against his chest as he held her.

"Ava, I...." He hesitated, not at all sure what he wanted to say.

"Shh." She pressed a finger to his lips. "I know. Me too."

It was too much too fast. Finding out Quinn was alive, almost getting mauled by a dog, and then standing there alone in the storm cellar with the only woman he'd ever truly loved in his arms. The questions swirling in his brain added to the confusion. Should he kiss her again? Did he want to? Would she want him to? Did he have a right to do so after the way he'd treated her for so long?

"Where did you guys go?" Angie asked from the kitchen, breaking the spell that had held them.

"Down here! Just getting some of your homemade soup to go with the sandwiches. I hope you don't mind!" Ava called up the stairs as she separated herself from Hudson's hold and headed back to the kitchen.

"Not at all! Just save the jar, please!" Angie's voice became softer as she must have walked away.

Hudson followed Ava up the stairs and closed the door to the pantry. Together they made sandwiches and warmed up the homemade soup. It felt to him like they were always meant to do things like that together. His mind moved back and forth between his realization that he might still love her and probably shouldn't have spent a decade wrapped up in anger aimed wrongly at her and the pictures of his sister that he'd basically abandoned ten years ago. Maybe he shouldn't have just accepted the investigation's determination of drowning. Perhaps he should have fought harder for more answers.

"Eli has a full belly and is sound asleep in your room, Ava. Bella wore herself out playing with him and is passed out on the playroom rug." Angie pulled out a chair and sat down at the table. "This looks delicious. Of course, you could put raw fish in front of me, and it would look good, since I didn't have to do a thing to prepare it!"

Ava laughed, a sound he realized he'd missed. "I'm glad you think so. Thank you for watching him."

Logan took the seat beside his wife, leaving just the chair next to Ava for Hudson.

"I'll say grace," Logan said, folding his hands in

prayer. "We thank you, Lord, for this food you've so graciously provided for us. And for the miracle that Hudson's little sister is alive. In your name, Amen."

"Amen," Ava said.

Hudson hadn't said grace before a meal or thanked God for anything in forever. It felt weird to do so, but he echoed Ava's sentiment. Thankful didn't begin to describe how he felt about finding Quinn.

"So," Logan said around a bite of sandwich, "I've called my cousins Keegan and Kaiden in for assistance tomorrow. They're both feds and know the ropes with cartel stuff better than any local cop."

"Won't there be jurisdictional issues?" Hudson asked after swallowing a spoonful of onion soup.

"This isn't an investigation. We aren't arresting anyone, and if we want to get your sister out of there alive, we need to sneak in—hopefully undetected, but I'm not counting on it—and pull her out."

"Technically, I'm on vacation, so I wouldn't have to worry about work," Hudson replied. "But what about the rest of you? I don't want anyone getting in trouble for anything."

Logan waved a hand in dismissal. "The James family men are like the wind—you never see them coming or going."

Angie choked, spitting out the milk she'd just

sipped. "Are you serious right now? 'Like the wind'? I gotta call Aunt Clara on that one."

"I'm sure they know what they're doing. I just don't want anyone to get hurt or in any trouble because of me." Hudson handed Angie his napkin. "I think you need this more than I do."

After they ate and cleaned up, Ava went to check on Eli, and Hudson headed outside to think. He needed a plan. Actually, several plans. One to rescue Quinn and another to figure out his feelings toward Ava. Or maybe to figure out hers toward him. He didn't even know if his feelings mattered at this point after how he'd treated her for so long.

As he sat on a bench near a small wildflower patch, he watched bees come and go from the various hives Logan tended. Their purpose seemed so simple: gather pollen, make honey, protect their queen. It made him a little envious that the tiny, fuzzy creatures had their lives mapped out so clearly when his map looked like a two-year-old had scribbled on a wall with a handful of crayons.

"Always so serious." Ava sat down beside him. "You should be joyful. Your sister is coming home soon."

He looked over at her, some of the happiness at finding Quinn dampened by shadows in her eyes.

"I'm sorry I didn't believe you. I'm sorry I didn't try harder to find her. How will Quinn ever forgive me?"

She stared ahead, maybe watching the bees the way he had. Maybe lost in her own thoughts about the situation. Eventually, she spoke again. "I've been thinking about that, and I wonder if maybe she didn't want to be found."

Hudson jumped up from the bench. "Is that why she kept Ricky a secret when they were dating? Because she'd planned to run away with him all along?"

Ava remained calm in the wake of his outburst. "I don't know. I mean, she could have found a way to reach out to one of us if she really wanted out. She found a way to get Eli out."

He paced the grass in front of the bench. "And now you have two known assassins trying to find you *and* Eli. I doubt it's just to check in on the little guy." He stopped pacing and let his shoulders droop in defeat. "There's just so much I don't know."

She reached out and touched his hand. "There's just so much *we* don't know. You're not in this alone, Hudson."

He turned his hand over so their palms pressed together. The warmth of her touch calmed him. He realized in that moment that his body's reaction to her had changed. He wasn't a clumsy teenager trying to steal a kiss anymore. They were adults, and his adult self recognized her soul as the match to his. Once he saved his sister, he really needed to figure out a way to make amends with Ava. He just prayed she'd let him.

Their little moments, like now or on the steps in the pantry, made him think she still had feelings for him. But, as he'd recently learned about himself, he'd become an expert in believing what he wanted and not necessarily what was true.

"I've missed her so much over the years, Ava." A stray tear escaped one eye, which he quickly brushed away. "It's just all so much to work through. What if you're right and she wants to be there? What if she won't leave?"

She shook her head, lightly tugging his hand to get him to sit back down. "I said I thought she hadn't wanted to be found. I think she does now. Something changed. And I'd bet a year's salary it has to do with Eli."

"You think so?" He hated how simultaneously hopeful and doubtful those words sounded.

"We'll know for sure tomorrow when we go after her, but yes, I do think so."

Her words sank in like a lead balloon. "You're not going with us tomorrow."

This time Ava jumped up. "What do you mean? I'm the only one who's actually seen her! You can't leave me out of it."

"I need you to be safe. I won't be able to concentrate on the mission if I'm also worried about you getting hurt."

She pointed at the scratch on his face. "You're the only one who got hurt today."

Her comment stoked his embarrassment, and it presented itself as anger. "You're not going, and that's final."

Ava huffed. Her voice went so quiet that he almost didn't hear her as she stomped off. "We'll see about that."

ELEVEN

Hudson had no right to exclude her from the rescue. She was the one who always knew Quinn was out there somewhere. She was the one who had a baby dropped off to her, and she was definitely the one people kept trying to attack—not to mention the fact that she was the one who found Quinn.

Nope. No way would she miss out on that.

Ava spent the rest of the day in the bedroom with Eli. When Angie offered dinner, she declined, and when Hudson finally came in to go to his room at bedtime, she pretended to be asleep. Her plan wouldn't work if he decided he wanted to talk about his feelings or something else utterly ridiculous at the moment.

It took a good long while for the house to go

silent. She really hoped their hosts weren't light sleepers. When she could hear snores coming from the den, Ava slid out of bed and slipped on her shoes. Angie had kindly left her some more clothes, so she wore more borrowed black leggings and a dark maroon long-sleeved shirt. Both would help keep her hidden. She'd tucked away the truck keys earlier in the day, so she fished those out of their hiding spot under her pillow and tiptoed to the bedroom door. Slipping quietly into the hall, she pulled the door shut even more softly and padded down the hall to the main entrance. She'd suspected the door to be a heavy steel, and it didn't disappoint as she dragged it open. Being extra careful not to let it slam closed behind her, she slowly allowed the latch to catch.

A full moon lit her way to the truck. Hudson had moved it over beside the detached garage. It sat facing the driveway. Ava did a little mental cheer; this meant she could put it in Neutral and let it roll down the hill until she had a bit of distance from the house. Hopefully, that would buy her the time she needed to get back to the compound where Quinn was being held before anyone noticed her absence.

Sliding behind the steering wheel of Hudson's truck, she adjusted the seat, then put the vehicle in Neutral and let it go. When she felt confident there was enough buffer area, she turned the key, and the engine roared to life.

When they'd driven out there that morning, Ava had noted directions on her phone. Opening them up, she turned the truck in the right direction and drove, never once looking back.

Finding Quinn and getting her out of that place had to be the only thing on her mind. There was no room to consider the obvious change in Hudson's attitude toward her, how much she'd enjoyed their brief kiss, or if she could even entertain another chance at a future with him.

Right then, all that mattered was her best friend, and if she didn't get her out of there before the guys headed over, there would be a huge mess to clean up.

The drive took less time than she thought it would. After parking the truck on the side of the road where Logan had earlier in the day, she locked it and hid the keys inside the back wheel well. She didn't want to risk dropping them anywhere, which would prevent their escape.

Following the same path they'd taken earlier, Ava headed to the rise she'd stood on before to scope out the property. A yellow-orange glow in the distance told her the entire compound was lit up like a landing strip at an airport. Getting in and out may be more difficult than she'd hoped for with so much security lighting. Using the light of the full moon to get her through the wooded area, she finally found the little hill she'd perched on earlier that day. From the same vantage point, she had a clear view of what appeared to be a bedroom wing. The lights that were on in a couple of the rooms revealed four-poster beds silhouetted in the windows.

Glancing around, she found a tree about twenty feet away that appeared to overhang the privacy wall. Ava had climbed plenty of trees in her day as a kid and spent years in gymnastics, so she felt confident she could manage that one. Grabbing a low-hanging branch, she hoisted herself to the first fork in the trunk and peered out over the compound. If she could get to the end of the limb and lower herself down, the drop wouldn't be far to the manicured lawn inside the wall—as long as she didn't turn an ankle with the dismount.

With precise movements mimicking her days on the balance beam, Ava slid out on the limb until she crossed the stone wall. Shifting her weight to one side, she lowered her body until she hung from the branch with her feet dangling about three feet above the ground. Fortunately, the limb was somewhat pliable and had bent just enough to make the drop less of a concern. Using one of her standard dismounts from her uneven bar days, she dropped to the ground without issue.

"Finally, all those years of training were useful in the real world." She straightened her clothes and redid the hair tie holding her curls back. "All right, now where are you, Quinn?"

Ava scanned the large grassy area, pausing at each window that still had a light on in the wee hours of the morning. She had to cross maybe forty yards undetected, and she had no idea exactly where she was headed. Ideally, Quinn would just be standing there in one of those windows so she'd know where to go.

Realizing her plan hadn't included *how* to find her friend, Ava crouched in the shadows to regroup. Her phone vibrated in the pocket of her leggings. That probably meant Hudson had discovered she was missing.

Pulling it out and looking at the screen confirmed it.

Where are you??

That one had been sent about thirty minutes earlier, followed by many more.

> Seriously, Ava. Answer me. Where are you?

> I'm getting worried. Please respond.

> You better not have gone back to the compound!

> You did, didn't you? My truck is gone.

> AVA!

Torn between putting it back in her pocket and letting him know she was okay, Ava finally typed out a quick text.

> I'm fine. Be back soon.

It was as vague as she could manage, but she knew Hudson would see right through it. That meant he'd probably come after her if he hadn't already, and the time she had left to rescue Quinn had just been severely limited. She shut off the phone and stowed it in her pocket once more.

Trying to stay in the shadows as much as possible, Ava worked her way across the expansive lawn until she could see more clearly. The large stone patio she'd seen Quinn standing on led to a wall of glass that provided a clear view into the spacious living area beyond. Despite all the lighting, no one appeared to be moving around inside. Even that horrible dog that had attacked Hudson seemed to have disappeared.

Moving as slowly and deliberately as she could, Ava made her way across the patio. About ten feet from the grassy area that was her destination, she caught the leg of a wrought iron chair with the toe of her shoe. The silent night air filled with the reverberations of iron scraping on stone. She froze, afraid to continue. Commotion inside the house caught her attention. She searched for a place to hide but found nothing. Running the rest of the way to the grass, she pressed herself flat against the building just as a bright floodlight turned on.

"Who's out there?" a man called out.

Ava's heart pounded, her pulse loud in her ears as she held her breath, knowing if they found her, the outcome wouldn't be good. In fact, her gut said it would be very, very bad.

"It was probably just a racoon or something," another man said. "Ain't no one getting in here unless we let 'em."

"I guess." The first man didn't sound convinced, but the light snapped off again.

Ava exhaled the breath she'd been holding and waited for her shaking legs to steady themselves.

It only took a minute for the adrenaline to recede so she could continue on in her mission. Praying that Quinn resided in a ground-floor bedroom, Ava moved along the stucco structure, stopping to peek in windows when she could.

At the very last window, she'd about given up hope that finding Quinn would be easy. Her mind raced, trying to figure out how to get inside the building without getting caught—or worse. The light was on, so she peeked in the corner of the last window just in case.

Her heart stuttered in her chest. Adrenaline bombarded her in a heavy rush as she saw the one person she'd thought she'd never see again, close enough to almost touch.

Quinn stood beside a tall bureau, brushing her long blonde hair.

Tears leaked from the corners of Ava's eyes. She blinked them away. No time for that now—she had to get Quinn's attention without startling her.

As best Ava could see, the only person in the room was her friend. Straightening, she reached up and tapped on the glass lightly. Quinn stopped brushing for a moment. Ava tapped again. Quinn walked over to the window, raising her hairbrush defensively as she peered outside. When she spotted

Ava, her eyes widened, and she slapped a hand over her mouth.

"Open the window," Ava whispered, motioning with her hands to mime the lifting of the sash.

Tossing the brush on the bed, Quinn then did just that. "Oh my gosh, Ava! Is it really you? I just knew you'd figure it out."

She pushed the screen up and leaned out the window, trying to wrap Ava in a hug, but Ava's lack of height made it nearly impossible. Laughing, Ava stepped out of the attempted embrace.

"Is it safe for me to climb in?"

Quinn eyed the distance to the ground. "Can you get up here?"

Ava grinned. "I've still got some gymnastics skills, apparently. How do you think I got over that wall?"

"Hold on." She watched as Quinn crossed the room and locked her door. On the return trip, she also turned off the two lamps.

Ava took a few steps back before running and leaping at the window like it was an old pommel horse. Quinn grabbed her under the arms and pulled her through. As soon as Ava got back on her feet, she found herself wrapped in a tight squeeze.

"I can't believe it's really you, Ava." Quinn held her briefly at arm's length. "You're so beautiful! Just like I remembered, only better. More grown-up, I suppose." She wrapped her arms around Ava again, holding her tight.

The tears fell freely. She didn't even try to hold back. They stayed that way, hugging and crying for a really long time. There were so many years of hugs to make up for.

Finally, they separated.

"How are you?" Ava asked. "Are you okay? What happened? I mean, ten years, Quinn. How have you been this close to Sunrise for so long and never come back?"

Quinn reached over and took her hands, squeezing them gently. "If I could have, I promise I would have. It just wasn't safe."

"For who? You? Eli?"

At the mention of the boy, Quinn's face lit up with joy. "I'm so glad you found him. He's amazing, isn't he?"

Her love for Eli made Ava smile. "He really is. But why did you abandon him? And how did you get him out of here?"

"I had no choice. He wasn't safe here. I didn't want him—" A shadow passed over Quinn's expression. "I knew you would take care of him." Her eyes lit up again. "I can't tell you how. Please don't ask me to." She glanced toward the door, a little bit of fear darkening her blue eyes. "I can't let you stay long, but I am so, so happy to see you."

She hugged Ava again. When Ava leaned forward, she felt the phone in her hip pocket. "I need to text Hudson." She turned on the phone and waited for it to boot up.

A new round of tears ran down Quinn's cheeks at the mention of her older brother. "How is Hudson?" She grabbed Ava's left hand and inspected it. "I thought for sure you two would be married by now!"

It was Ava's turn for the shadows. "Not quite. We haven't spoken much since you went missing. Except during the last couple days, anyway. He was the responding officer to finding Eli at the church."

Quinn's eyes widened. "My brother is a *cop*? I never would have imagined him going down that road."

"I know, right?" Ava laughed.

A loud rapping on the door startled them both. Quinn held a finger to her lips as she got off the bed. "What do you want?"

"I heard voices. What's going on in there?"

Ava sucked in a breath. The voice—it sounded just like one of the men who had broken into her office.

"I had the television on. Sorry if it was too loud. I couldn't sleep," Quinn said through the door.

"Yeah, well, turn it down. You don't want the boss waking up. He won't be too happy about it."

"Okay. Sorry again."

They listened as heavy footsteps retreated down the hall. Quinn collapsed against the door, stifling a giggle.

Ava didn't find any of it to be funny. "Who was that?" she asked, her voice barely above a whisper.

"One of Rosario's men. Security."

"He stalked me and tried to kill me. More than once. Also ransacked my office, stole my laptop, smashed a window in my house, and shot up Hudson's truck and house. He's not in security."

"It's a different type of security, I guess." Quinn's eyes filled with tears. "I'm really sorry about all that."

Ava's phone began to vibrate. She ignored it, but it happened again. And then again. Finally grabbing it and looking at the screen, she saw a dozen or so texts from Hudson.

The last few made her worry.

If you don't call me, we are going to storm the entire compound looking for you.

In ten minutes.

Come on, Ava. Logan and I saw my truck. I know you're around here somewhere.

CALL ME.

"Your brother is very annoying." Ava held up the phone so Quinn could see the litany of messages. "We need to get out of here so he and his friend don't get themselves killed."

The fear that shone on Quinn's face when she mentioned leaving shocked Ava.

"I can't leave. He'll find me and kill me. Then he'll find you and Hudson and Eli and have you all killed too."

"That won't happen. Hudson won't let it." She grabbed her friend's hand. "Come on. Let's go."

Quinn backed away, tears streaming down her cheeks. "No. Please. You better go. I already won't be able to live with myself for dragging you into this mess."

Ava held up both her hands in surrender. "It's okay. I'm sorry. I didn't mean to upset you." She pulled up Hudson's number on the phone. "I'm going to call him so he won't do anything stupid. Then we'll figure this out together."

Her friend shook her head. "There's nothing to figure out. You have to leave. *Please.*"

Quinn turned and disappeared into the bathroom.

There was absolutely no way Ava would be leaving that room without her best friend. Not when she could hear the heartbreaking sobs on the other side of the bathroom door. She had the distinct feeling that there was so much more to the story of Quinn's last ten years than she could ever guess. She hit Send on the call and waited for Hudson to answer.

He did so on the first ring. "Ava!" She could hear the frantic fear in his voice.

"I'm fine, Hudson. More than fine, actually. I found Quinn."

"Is she with you? Can I talk to her?" The frantic fear instantly became frantic hope.

"Um...." Ava tried to come up with a good excuse as to why he couldn't speak to Quinn just yet. Finally, she settled on the truth. Sort of. "She's in the bathroom."

"Bathroom? Where exactly are you, Ava?" She could hear that fear returning to his voice.

"Well, funny story. I'm actually inside the compound, in Quinn's bedroom."

"What!" She swore she heard him hit something. "Are you insane?"

"No!" Ava realized too late that she'd shouted the word.

"Logan and I are coming in there."

"Don't. We're fine. We'll be leaving soon. I don't need your help. It'll just put you in danger."

A loud crash sounded behind her as the bedroom door flew open in a flurry of splintering wood and slammed into the wall. "Freeze!"

"Um, Hudson? I might actually need some help now."

SEVERAL GUNSHOTS PUNCTUATED AVA'S request for help before the call went silent. The panic that lodged in his throat as the only connection between them dropped nearly suffocated him. News that his sister was alive and well had filled him with hope. What he'd just heard destroyed it all.

Logan had gone around the front of the compound while Hudson stood on the hill Ava had discovered at the back earlier in the day. Knowing his sister and the woman he definitely still loved were inside that house with criminals and killers cut him to the core. Panic threatened to overtake reason as he resisted the urge to storm the front door and tear through the massive building. Climbing a nearby tree, he shimmied out onto the lowest limb until he'd cleared the stone wall and dropped into the massive yard below. Unholstering his weapon, he then held it ready as he started a perimeter walk toward the front of the building. With any luck, he'd run into Logan, and if he didn't, then it would be a solo mission because he had absolutely no intention of leaving there without the two most important people in his world.

If they were even still alive. He'd counted five gunshots. Those odds scared him even more.

His phone vibrated in his pocket. Checking the screen, he saw a message from Logan.

Dude, where are you?

After ducking into a shadow behind a tall shrub, he typed a reply.

Ava called. She's with Quinn somewhere inside. I heard gunshots. Going in after them.

He didn't even get to put the phone back in his pocket before a call came in. "Hello?"

"Don't go in there alone. Tell me where you are.

I'll go too." Logan sounded out of breath, like he'd been running to find Hudson.

"No way, man. Angie'd kill me if I let you die. I've got this one on my own."

"Seriously, Hud. Let me go with you. You're going to need backup. Have you seen all the armed men in there?"

There was no way he'd tell Logan where he was. Angie scared him. In her former life as an NYPD cop, she'd taken on the mob and won. He couldn't imagine what she'd do to him if her husband got hurt, let alone killed.

"Nope. What I really need is to get through the front door. If there are two of us, it'll be much harder to sneak past. Can you find someplace high enough to see over the gate and provide cover fire if I need it?"

Logan exhaled loudly. Hudson knew that meant he wasn't too happy about it, but he'd agree. "Fine. But if an all-out gun battle starts, I'm coming in. Angie scares me, too, brother. If I didn't do something to help, I'd be better off going to live with my aunt Clara because Angie'll kick my ass."

Hudson chuckled quietly. He'd met Aunt Clara one time, and she wouldn't be any easier on Logan if he messed up. "Okay, deal. But I'll be fine. In and out.

It's, like, three in the morning. How many people could be awake, anyway?"

"Pretty much everyone after those gunshots," Logan said. "Be careful, Hud. And if you get in trouble, call. I'll be there."

Hudson nodded, even though his friend obviously couldn't see him. "Thanks, I will." Probably he wouldn't. No sense in them both dying over Quinn and Ava when he didn't even know if *they* were still alive.

He disconnected the call and dropped the phone back in his pocket before he proceeded to make his way to the circular drive in front of the home. With any luck, one of the cars would be open, and he would find a jacket or something he could use to further blend in.

Somewhere in the distance, an owl hooted as a cloud passed in front of the full moon. The whole thing gave him an ominous feeling that he was about to make a huge mistake. But what choice did he have? He'd failed Quinn once; he wouldn't be doing that again, even if it only meant a body to properly bury this time. And Ava? Well, he had a lot to atone for on that front. If she'd ever let him try.

As he got closer to the driveway, he moved more cautiously. Cameras seemed to be everywhere, and the last thing he needed was to have an overzealous security guard shooting at him blindly.

Loud voices echoed from the house. Hudson's pulse pounded in his arteries. The odds of him getting in and out unnoticed were just about nonexistent.

Crouching, he tried the door handle of the first car, praying there wouldn't be an alarm. Finding it locked, he moved on to the second one. That door opened, but he found nothing useful inside it. With only one vehicle left, the third time just had to be the charm.

Tugging the back passenger door handle, he held his breath, half expecting a shrill car alarm to sound. Instead, the door opened quietly. Letting out the air he'd been holding, Hudson peered into the back seat of the car.

"Jackpot," he whispered, grabbing a dark-colored baseball hat and a matching windbreaker off the seat. Closing the door quietly, he then slipped into the jacket and pulled the hat down low over his eyes. Another check of the area told him he was still alone outside—for the moment, anyway.

Sticking to the shadows as much as the full moon would let him, he inched his way toward the main entrance of the house. From the corner of one eye, he caught a flash of something. Hoping it was Logan moving to a vantage point, Hudson pushed forward until he made it behind some bushes near the front door. After taking a moment to regroup and whisper yet another prayer for safety, he took a deep breath and stepped onto the porch. In full view of several cameras, he reached out and tried the door handle. It moved.

Please don't let an alarm be set.

With his heart pounding in his chest, he pulled the door open, then waited for an alarm, a hailstorm of bullets, or some other indicator that he'd been discovered. Nothing happened. Based on shadows he saw falling across the foyer, he knew several people were milling around in the next room. In an effort to look like he belonged there, Hudson put his gun in the pocket of the windbreaker and boldly walked into the massive entryway. He closed the door behind him and took a moment to look around, orienting himself.

Huge polished columns rose to the ceiling that sported a mural of the sky. The lone raven that had been painted on a branch facing the door gave him a chill. Its glittering black eyes were so lifelike, he would have thought it were alive if he didn't know better. Directly across the huge open space was a wall of glass. Floor-to-ceiling windows and a couple of large sliding glass doors provided a perfect view of a garden that surrounded a huge elaborate fountain that was the main focal piece. Under any other circumstance, Hudson would have been intrigued with the outdoor area. It resembled the sort of sanctuary he'd been trying to create in his own yard. For the moment, though, his focus had to be entirely on his reason for being there.

Several different voices sounded from the back of the house and seemed to get quieter and more distant the longer he listened. Worried what that might mean for Quinn and Ava, he worked to keep his calm as he surveyed the surroundings. He really just wanted to tear through the mansion until he found the women, but years of training told him to do it right, for their safety and his.

Hallways ran from either side of the foyer. The one to the left contained the windows where lights had been on when Ava called him. As he moved in that direction, his footsteps barely made a sound against the shiny marble floor.

The hall was brightly lit for the early morning hours. It appeared he'd chosen the bedroom wing, and with all the open doors and lights on, he assumed he had to be headed in the correct direction. As he tiptoed along, he listened for any sign that Quinn and Ava were nearby, but he heard nothing.

When he finally reached the end of the hall, he found one more door that stood ajar. A familiar scent wafted out of the room beyond. It was the way his sister used to smell. She loved floral fragrances that were light and would fill a room but not be too over-powering.

Gripping his gun, Hudson pushed the door open wider with his elbow and looked around inside. He barely noticed the large four-poster bed covered in throw pillows of every shade of purple or the large dresser with a picture of Quinn and some man he didn't recognize. The distinctly feminine space that echoed his sister's entire personality hardly sank in at all. The only thing he could focus on was the large spot of dark red liquid on the white area rug.

Forgetting to be quiet, he dashed inside and ran to the bathroom. The large tiled space with the claw-foot tub and glass-enclosed shower held no sign of anyone. Stepping back into the bedroom, he glanced around quickly. One window stood open with its screen lifted. The other two on either side of it were closed and locked. Stepping up to the window, he checked the ledge and frame, then stuck his upper body outside and looked at the ground below. There were definitely footsteps in the damp grass, but they led to the window, not away.

He turned and looked at the floor. The wet spot on the rug had a tiny trail of droplets leading away from it toward the bedroom door. That could mean whoever was injured had possibly walked out of the room.

Hudson moved over to the dresser and picked up the framed picture. Quinn seemed so happy on the surface, but if he looked a little deeper, he could have sworn he saw shadows of sadness in her blue eyes.

Tracing the outline of the frame with one fingertip, he studied the man who stood beside her. Young and good-looking with dark features and a smile he didn't quite trust.

"I'm so sorry, baby sister. I should have looked for you. I should have known, somehow, that you were still alive."

He turned the frame over and took the back out before slipping the photo of Quinn from it—just in case it was all he'd have left. Tucking it into his back pocket, he took one last glance around the room, then followed the blood drops out into the hall, thankful he hadn't smudged them on his way down to the room. The trail took him back to the main entryway. He continued to follow them through the kitchen.

"Where on earth did you get to?" he said quietly as the drops suddenly stopped near a large stainless steel sink.

"Hey! Who are you?" someone yelled from across the room.

Hudson jumped, then spun around to see the man holding a gun that was pointed straight at him.

He held his hands up in front of him. "Hey, man, don't shoot. I'm just looking for a snack."

Maybe the other guy would believe he just didn't know him and let Hudson go on his way.

The man took a couple steps closer. "Hey! That's my jacket!"

Of course it was.

Hudson backed away slowly, maintaining eye contact with the guy. "I think you're mistaken."

The man stepped forward. "I don't think I am. That's also my hat you're wearing."

Hudson spotted a door about twenty feet away that he really hoped led outside.

"Well, if you want it back, here it is." He grabbed the hat from his head and flung it at the other man's face. The hat must have made hard contact, based on the shout he heard as he turned and ran to the door.

A shot fired, the bullet slamming into the wall above his head as he yanked the door open and ran out into the darkness. Several more shots sounded, at least two passing close enough that Hudson heard them whiz by. He zigzagged over the lawn, trying to be a harder target to hit. Shouting filled the night as more guns were fired in his direction. He spotted a series of outbuildings up ahead. Giving it all he had, he covered the rest of the distance to the first one but kept on going in between them, keeping to the shadows. The shouting got louder as the men pursued him. Ducking into one of the small sheds, he searched for a place to hide but found nothing.

Making sure they hadn't caught up to him yet, Hudson slipped back out of the shed and ran toward what looked like a multicar garage. The side door wasn't locked when he tried the knob. Inside the garage were several dark sedans like the ones in the driveway. About halfway across the space, he saw a hatch in the ceiling. If he could get up there, the crawlspace would provide a decent hiding spot. He could hear voices getting steadily louder.

Time to move.

One of the cars was parked directly below it. Hudson stepped up on the back bumper, eyeing the distance to the hatch from the roof of the car. Deciding he could definitely pull himself up, he climbed to the top of the vehicle and pushed on the little door in the ceiling. It popped up easily and slid to the side. He grabbed the ledge on either side, took a deep breath, bent his knees, and pushed upward. His arms burned as he pulled his body up, but he managed to get high enough to fall forward onto the floor of the space and pull himself the rest of the way.

As he slid the hatch cover closed, someone flipped a switch, flooding the garage in bright incandescent light. Hudson left a tiny crack so he could see what was happening below. At least a little bit of it, anyway.

"See anything?" someone asked.

"No. Check all the cars, though. He could be hiding in or under one of them," a second man replied.

A radio crackled. The second voice said, "Yeah?"

"Boss wants to know is it safe? Can he get to his car okay?" The radio crackled some, but Hudson could still make out the voice coming through.

"Yeah, I think so. Bill just checked all the cars. No sign of the guy." Someone stepped into view. Hudson sucked in a breath. The last time he'd seen that guy, he'd had a gun pointed at Hudson in his living room.

It took large amounts of self-control not to give himself away by jumping down and punching the guy in the face. He knew that would give him momentary pleasure but not long-term satisfaction. No, he had to focus on finding Ava and Quinn and getting them out of there.

"All right. Boss is headed that way."

Where could Rosario Baron be headed in the early hours of the morning? Hudson could hear the men talking, but they'd moved somewhere that made it hard for him to make out what they were actually saying.

His phone vibrated in his pocket. He'd forgotten all about Logan! Careful not to make any noise, he pulled out his phone.

Hey, man, you okay? Heard a lot of shots fired.

He quickly typed a response.

I'm good. Don't come after me. I'll text if I need you. Stay safe.

Logan's response was brief.

10-4.

The space around him was cluttered with abandoned furniture, random car parts, and dusty tools. Obviously, the attic was where discarded items went to fade away into the past. The floor shook as one of the garage doors opened. The car next to the one he'd climbed onto turned on, the engine roaring to life.

"Have all the arrangements been made?" A deep male voice that he'd not heard before asked the question. He sounded older, more refined.

"Yes, sir." The one who'd shot at Hudson at his house stepped into view again. "The plane has been fueled, and the pilot is on standby at the field."

"Excellent. My family in Spain have been notified of my arrival and that I'll have guests?"

Hudson assumed it was Rosario Baron speaking. When the older man moved into sight, it confirmed his hunch.

"Yes, boss. They have been notified and look forward to your arrival."

Rosario nodded. "Very good. You'll be driving us to the airport."

"Absolutely, sir. Whatever you need."

If Rosario left the compound, Hudson could have more freedom to search for Ava and Quinn. He just had to wait until the garage emptied out. As he watched the men milling around, he was completely unprepared for what he saw next.

Quinn and Ava, both with their hands secured behind them, walked into his sightline with a man holding a gun behind them. Ava had blood smeared on one side of her face, and Quinn's blonde hair was a mess, but other than that, they looked like they were both okay.

The urge to call out welled up in his throat and very nearly succeeded in asserting itself. He held back, though, knowing if he said or did anything, he could put them both in very serious danger. Instead, he tried to focus on the fact that they were both *alive*, something he hadn't been at all sure of after seeing the blood in Quinn's bedroom. Pulling his phone back out, he typed a text to Logan.

> Quinn and Ava in black sedan about to leave for local airfield. Destination Spain. We have to stop them.

Logan's reply came fast.

> I'll follow in my truck. Can you find wheels?

He'd hotwire a car if he had to.

> Yeah. I'll catch up. Don't wait.

"Get in the car." Gun guy herded Quinn and Ava into the back seat of the running sedan.

"You don't have to be so pushy," Ava snapped.

That made Hudson smile. Even in a life-or-death situation, she still didn't let anyone tell her what to do without a fight.

"Just do it, Ava."

It was the first time he'd heard his sister's voice in a decade, and she sounded so sad and so resigned. What had they done to her? Quinn had been a fighter. She never took anything from anyone. The anger he'd felt building since first finding out she'd been alive all along reared up a little more.

Once the women had gotten into the back of the sedan, Rosario Baron sat in the front passenger seat while the guy who'd shot up his house got into the driver's seat.

At least three other guys who Hudson had seen milling around piled into a second car, and that engine roared to life, echoing through the enclosed space. The garage door directly in front of that car opened, and they pulled out into the dark.

The car carrying his sister and Ava followed. Both doors closed, but the lights remained on.

Hudson inched the hatch door open a bit wider and shifted so he could see more of the space below. With no sign of any other men, he stuck his head down a little farther just as the lights shut off, cloaking the garage in darkness. He turned and hung his feet out of the opening, then lowered himself to the top of the car below. Quickly stepping off the vehicle, he jumped into the car, found a garage-door opener, and pushed it. As the door opened, the overhead lights came on again. He fully expected to hear bullets being fired at him, but everything remained quiet aside from the pounding of his pulse in his ears. Thinking he'd have to hotwire the car, he was shocked to find the keys in the cupholder of the console.

Hudson had no idea where the local airfield was, so he quickly asked the onboard GPS. In a few seconds, he sped out of the garage and down the long drive toward the front of the compound.

The gate stood open when he arrived, thankfully. Someone must have seen him coming and thought he was a Baron henchman. GPS said to turn left, so he did as he was told, barely slowing down. The back end of the car kicked out as the wheels attempted to grab hold of the pavement. Hudson floored the gas pedal, and the tires spun in a cloud of burning rubber as he lurched forward and raced down the road.

TWELVE

Ava could feel Quinn trembling in the seat beside her. She'd heard her captors discussing an international flight, which was a very bad thing for her and Quinn. Once they were out of the country, they might be lost forever. She had to figure a way out before that plane took off.

"Quinn," she whispered, "are you okay?"

Her friend looked at her with so much sadness in her eyes that it made her heart ache. "I want to go home."

Did she mean the compound or home to Sunrise?

"Where are you taking us?" Ava raised her voice so there'd be no mistaking that she wanted the men up front to hear.

The one she'd learned was Rosario Baron, head of

the cartel, turned to look at her. With a smile more evil than friendly, he gave a little wave of his hand. "On a trip."

"But *where*?"

"Overseas." He turned back around, obviously dismissing any more questions.

"This is kidnapping. Quinn's brother is a cop. You won't get away with it."

Both men laughed at that. Rosario didn't even bother to look at her when he replied. "Ah, yes. The infamous brother I've heard so much about recently. If the FBI, Interpol, and every other international law enforcement agency couldn't get to me, what makes you think a local cop in a rinky-dink little town will be able to?"

"You don't know Hudson!" Apparently, Quinn's outburst definitely caught them all off guard.

Rosario turned back to look at her, his dark eyes full of anger. "And you don't know *me*. You have no idea what I am truly capable of. In fact, you know very little."

He left those last few words hanging in the air, the threat behind them quite evident. Perhaps it was even more of a promise of what would come if they got on that plane.

"I know Ricky loved me! Something you are absolutely incapable of understanding!"

Rosario narrowed his eyes at Quinn. Something in his expression chilled Ava straight to the bone. "Do not presume to know anything about me, young lady. You have no concept of the way I felt for my son. Nor did you fully understand the power my son had. In our world, you are nothing. I accepted you because my son loved you, but he is gone now."

"Of course he is! You killed him!" Quinn broke down into loud sobs, ugly crying in a way Ava had never witnessed from her before.

"I did not kill my only child." The chill emanating from Rosario Baron scared Ava.

"You made sure you sent him off somewhere that would get him killed! All because you couldn't stand him having me and our baby in his life. He couldn't be at your beck and call anymore."

Mucus ran from Quinn's nose, her face was soaked in tears, and she had never looked so sure of herself in their entire friendship. Apparently, her father-in-law did not agree.

"Ricky understood the rules of our family. Something you never have."

Ever since Ava had been discovered in Quinn's room, confidence that Hudson would find them warred with the fear that he wouldn't. For the first time, that fear felt like an advantage. It was up to her to figure out how to get them away from there before they were shipped overseas like cargo.

Human cargo.

It clicked in her brain. Logan and Hudson had said Rosario was suspected to be a top player in the human trafficking business. All of a sudden, she knew exactly what they planned to do with her and Quinn.

Trying not to be too obvious, she worked the zip tie on her wrists, trying to loosen it even just a little bit. If she could get her hands free, she would have a better chance of saving them.

"There's someone behind us," the driver said to Rosario. "They're moving in fast."

"Lose them." Rosario's voice had turned ice-cold. All business. That worried Ava a whole lot more.

The sedan lurched forward as the driver slammed the gas pedal down. The force threw Ava and Quinn against the seat in front of them, tumbling them both to the floor. The vehicle behind them sped up as well; Ava could tell by the brightness of the headlights in the interior. Maybe Hudson had come for them after all.

The sedan suddenly took a right turn way too fast,

based on the squeal of the tires and the way the back end of the car fishtailed, throwing her and Quinn against each other. Another forceful turn tossed her around a little more, snapping the zip ties that bound her wrist.

Thank God! Now if she could get Quinn free....

A sharp curve must have come up out of nowhere. The driver let out a few curse words as he struggled to keep the car on the road. Quinn's body jerked sideways, making her smack her head against the armrest on the door. She immediately went limp.

"Quinn!" Ava whisper-shouted as she shook her friend. Quinn remained unconscious.

"I think I lost him, boss. It looks like he went off the road into the trees back there."

"Good. Now get us to the plane. Immediately."

"Yes, sir."

Ava stayed put on the floor of the car. No one even seemed to care that they were still back there. The driver turned left down a narrow, roughly paved road. The night, now even darker due to the canopy of trees overhead, made everything seem ominous. The trees would provide cover if they could somehow get out of the car, though, and that was where her focus had to be.

If only Quinn would wake up. They could probably jump from the vehicle with little injury at the slower speed it traveled at the moment. She refused to leave her friend behind, though, so concentrating on reviving Quinn had to be her priority. If she'd even wake up. A bad enough concussion could require treatment. New levels of panic added to Ava's existing fears.

As she tried to figure out what to do next, the driver spoke again. "Uh, boss? We have company again."

She peeked up over the back seat and spotted headlights in the distance.

"I thought you said the driver went off the road." Rosario shifted to look behind them.

Ava stayed still on the floor, trying to be invisible and forgotten about.

"He did. I think this is a different vehicle. The headlights have a different glow."

"Lose it. I've had enough of this. We have to get on that plane before the sun rises."

Rosario Baron's tone gave her a chill that went straight to her bones. When he put his window down and started shooting at the car behind them, Ava's heart practically dropped into her stomach.

The car plowed forward, bouncing and creaking as it hit pothole after pothole. Ava was slammed against the floorboards over and over again as they picked up speed. Holding Quinn's hand, she sent up multiple prayers begging God to protect them while the car raced along the road.

All of a sudden, there was a loud creak followed by the driver letting out a yell. "Hold on, boss! We lost a wheel! We're gonna roll!"

The car veered sharply to the right. Ava sucked in a breath, mentally preparing for what was about to happen. She briefly considered covering her friend with her own body, but the idea was nixed for her. As the sedan hit the dirt and rocks at the side of the road, the axle must have caught on something. A terrible grinding filled the car, punctuated by her own screams. They were launched into the air. Ava closed her eyes, she and Quinn tumbling around each other as the car rolled once, twice, and then a third time. Windows exploded, covering them in shattered glass while the shriek of metal scraping along the decline pierced her eardrums painfully. As the car took one last tumble, finally crashing into a stand of trees, Ava was tossed out the back window. She landed on her back, the wind completely knocked from her lungs.

The trees above her moved gently in the night

breeze. A loud ringing filled her ears as she gasped for air. When she could breathe again, Ava rolled to one side and tried to process what had happened. From what she could tell, the car had landed on the driver's side, the bottom of it smashing against the trunks of several trees. Not far from where she was, Rosario Baron lay with his head at a very unnatural angle.

The pungent scent of petroleum surrounded her. The gas tank must have ruptured. A slight hint of something burning penetrated the gasoline smell. Ava sat straight up, ignoring the fact that every inch of her body hurt beyond words.

"Fire! Quinn! You need to get out of there!"

"Ava?"

The single word was so faint she couldn't even be sure she'd actually heard her friend say it. Ava scrambled clumsily to the car and looked through the same long window she'd fallen out of. She spotted Quinn in a crumpled heap against the back driver-side door.

"I'm coming, Quinn! Hang on, sister!"

Flames had begun to rise from the underside of the car. It wouldn't take long for the entire area to be engulfed.

Crawling through glass and other debris, she tugged Quinn's arms to get her into a position where she could haul her out. The flames grew, the smoke thickened, and the heat kicked up all around them.

"I can do this." The little pep talk she offered to herself didn't do much to boost her confidence as she shifted Quinn enough to get a hold of her under her arms and pull. She pulled once more, using the back of the car seat for leverage, but Quinn didn't move.

"Are you stuck?" she asked as she felt around in the smoke-filled cabin of the car. Quinn made no response. As she said the words, her fingers came across something that had a sharp edge, and Quinn's pajamas were caught on it.

The crackling of the fire roared in her ears, and the flames licked at the front of the seat Quinn was jammed behind. Ava tugged the pajama pants so hard, the fabric ripped, releasing her friend. She yanked as hard as she could, pulling Quinn's still-lifeless body out of the car. As the flames consumed the entire interior of the vehicle, Ava dragged her friend to the shadows and safety of several trees about thirty feet away, where she collapsed on the ground, gasping for air.

Shifting so she could rest her head on her friend's shoulder, Ava reached over and squeezed the other woman's hand. "You're free now, Quinn. You and Eli are free."

The car exploded, sending a massive fireball up into the air and raining embers down all around them. A severed arm, she assumed from the driver, landed about three feet away, the pungent odor of burnt flesh causing her to gag. The heat closed in as the smoke blanketed them. Every breath became a challenge.

"I'm sorry, Hudson. I really tried." Ava let her eyes close, grateful they'd survived the car wreck but not so certain she'd saved anyone.

THE WINDSHIELD SUDDENLY CRACKED ACROSS the entire surface as something flew past his right ear. In the center of the glass, there was a small hole. A few dings to the front end and a headlight explosion confirmed his worst fear. "Someone is shooting at us! Are you hit?"

"Nah, I'm good! The back seat might have a nice hole in it, though."

Hudson slammed the brakes on the car, nearly spinning around in a cloud of dust. "Did you see that?"

"Yeah." Logan waved his hand forward. "Get there. Now!"

No one had to tell him twice. Hudson hit the gas, flooring the pedal and sending the sedan flying down the road that was pitted with rocks and deep depressions. His grip on the steering wheel made his knuckles ache. Thankfully, the shooting stopped. Which also concerned him. A man like Rosario Baron wouldn't leave a job undone. He'd fire his weapon until the bitter end.

Hudson tried to refocus on the mission and not worry about why the shooting stopped. After he'd found Logan walking along the side of the road a few miles back, his buddy bruised and scraped from wrecking his vehicle during the pursuit, he'd been certain they would be too late to stop the plane. When they'd turned down the back road Logan said would get them to the runway faster, Hudson's hope returned at the sight of taillights a mile or so ahead of them. The driver of the vehicle must have suspected they were after them because the car suddenly sped up to a level far too dangerous for that road. Hudson did his best to keep up without putting them in danger. As he closed the distance, something came at them in the road, rolling out of the dark into the illumination of his one working headlight.

A car tire.

His gut knotted. Losing a wheel at that kind of

speed would be very, very bad. No wonder the shooting had stopped.

As they drove toward the last place where he'd seen the red glow of taillights, Hudson pushed away at the panic and focused on finding the crippled vehicle.

"Hudson." Logan pointed up ahead and off to the side. "That looks like the glow of fire."

"Oh, God. *No.*" He slammed the gas pedal to the floor. All he could think about was his sister and the woman he loved trapped in that car. They needed him, and that was what mattered.

Logan braced himself against the door handle and the dash. "Hole!" he'd shout every so often as he spotted a dip or pothole up ahead.

As they got closer to the suspected fire, smoke filled the air, confirming Hudson's worst fear. He spotted the tread marks just ahead where the driver had hit the brakes and slid the vehicle sideways. Broken branches and trampled brush indicated the path the car had taken down the hill.

He slammed his own brakes, sliding the sedan a ways off into the breakdown area. As they jumped out of the car, a huge explosion shook the ground and sent a giant ball of fire barreling into the night sky.

"Ava! Quinn!" Hudson half ran and half slid down

the damp ground toward where the fire was. Logan followed closely.

As they neared the fire, he could make out the outline of a car. Or what was left of it. He ran to it, yelling over and over again. "Quinn! Ava! Where are you! I'm here!" Spotting an opening in the flames, he dove toward the car. "Ava!"

Strong arms yanked him back and tossed him to the ground. "You're on fire, man! Roll!"

Logan beat at him with the shirt he'd been wearing, trying to put out the flames as Hudson did as he was told, rolling the way they'd taught him in grade school. He could almost hear his third-grade teacher's voice in his head.

"What do you do if your clothes catch on fire? Stop! Drop! Roll!"

When he no longer felt the heat of his clothes melting into his skin, he stopped. Lying on his back, exhausted and in pain, he looked at his friend through the tears in his eyes. "I have to get them out of there."

Logan jerked his head as he tried to shake ash and dirt out of his shirt. "I'm so sorry, dude. It's too late. The car is *gone*. Like, incinerated. There's no way either of them could have survived that."

Hudson forced himself to sit up, his body

screaming at him as the fabric of his clothes pulled away from his skin, burnt tissue clinging to it and ripping from his arms and torso. "I've got to try!"

As he stumbled to his feet, then fell forward, Logan caught him in a light bear hug. "Look at me, Hud." Logan waited for him to actually look up. "It's too late. They're gone."

"No!" He turned his head up to the sky. "How could You do this to me again? Trust God. Believe. Have faith. That's all anyone has said to me for ten years! I finally start to think there is a chance You might exist, and then You let this happen!"

"None of this is His fault!" Logan held him by the arms above the burned areas. "And it's not your fault either! It's their fault." He waved toward the car. "The men who took them are to blame. I won't let you blame yourself anymore!"

The tears came then. A week ago, he'd have walked away, forced the tears and the accompanying emotions to the dark recesses of his mind. But he had no more fight in him. No more strength to act like everything was just fine. He sobbed like a baby, dropping to the ground as his body burned and his heart broke. Logan just stood there and let him have his moment. Honestly, Hudson barely noticed his friend was there as he yelled, cried, and yelled some more.

His entire life, since the day his parents died on the ocean in the hurricane, Hudson had held his emotions in check. Whether it was the adrenaline, sadness, or pain that won, he didn't even care. As far as he was concerned in that moment, he'd had enough of life and just hoped the fire would come close enough to put him out of his misery.

"Help. Please, help us."

The call was so quiet, he couldn't even be sure he'd heard it. Logan looked confused, as though he may have been thinking the same thing.

"Did you hear it too?" Hudson asked.

His friend shrugged. "Someone calling for help?"

Hudson nodded and dragged himself back to his feet. "Is someone out there?"

"Help us! She's unconscious. I can't move her."

"That's Quinn. Logan! I hear Quinn!" If someone had told him to his face that he was wrong, he wouldn't have believed them. He'd know his sister's voice anywhere. "Where are you? We can't tell which direction you are over the fire."

"Here! We're here! Is that you, Hudson? Oh my God, Hudson! Help us!"

Logan pointed at the woods. "I think she's in there."

"Yes! It's me! Keep talking! We're coming!" Hudson shouted.

"We're here. Ava is with me, but she won't wake up! I don't even know if she's alive. I can't find a pulse!" Quinn's voice cracked.

They ran through the trees and brush. Prickly branches grabbed at Hudson's burns, but he barely noticed. "I'm coming, Quinn!"

About thirty feet into the woods, he found both the most beautiful and heart-wrenching sight he'd ever seen. Quinn was sitting on the ground, her face streaked with blood, dirt, and smoke, her blonde hair wild and tangled around her. Ava lay in her lap, her clothes also muddy and torn, her face covered in dirt and blood as well.

"Quinn! You're alive!" He ran to her and dropped down to wrap her in a hug that pulled at all his wounds, but he couldn't care less.

"Hudson! You're hurt!" Quinn looked at his burned arms in horror.

"It's nothing. I'm fine." It was a total lie, but he hardly cared.

"Help Ava! Please!"

He turned his attention to the woman he'd sworn for over a decade he didn't need in his life. Seeing her lifeless body lying there screamed at him how wrong he'd been for so long. He needed her. He loved her. And it might be too late to tell her.

Logan had already started compressions. "I don't feel a pulse. How long has she been out like this?"

Quinn shook her head. "I don't know. I just woke up a few seconds ago. I think I hit my head. I have no idea how any of this happened." She let out a sob as tears ran down her cheeks.

"Let me do it." He pushed Logan aside and started chest compressions on Ava. "You go get help."

Quinn's face lit up. "Here!" She pulled her cell phone from her pocket and handed it to Logan. "You can call 9-1-1!"

Logan took the phone and made the call. Quinn sat beside Hudson, alternating between laughing hysterically and crying.

Hudson focused on the CPR he was performing. Tunnel vision set in, and all he could see was Ava's lifeless body and all the ways he'd hurt her since Quinn first disappeared. "Come on, Ava. Breathe. I need you to breathe, baby. I love you. Please."

At some point he felt Logan replacing his hands and continuing the chest compressions as he lay down on the ground beside Ava, his last thought that at least he would die with the woman he loved if he couldn't be alive with her.

From some distant place, he heard Quinn's voice and felt her squeeze his hand. The pain and terror and exhaustion washed over him as the adrenaline pushed through his system until things just faded to black.

Is this what it feels like to die?

THIRTEEN

Ava swiped at the thing on her face. As it shifted to the side, she felt a rush of cool air come out of it. She opened her eyes to an unfamiliar room. The gentle glow of lights and quiet but for the constant beeping confirmed she was in a hospital room. At least she wasn't dead.

Unless Quinn was dead. Then maybe she didn't really want to be alive. How would she ever face Hudson again if she hadn't managed to save his sister for a second time? She knew Quinn's disappearance all those years ago wasn't her fault, but this one—this would totally be on her. She'd gone off half-cocked, thinking she could take on one of the most powerful criminals in the world and win.

Of course, she almost had won. She'd believed her friend was still alive and found her when no one else had. But she'd gone and gotten them kidnapped, and then there was the car wreck. And the fire. She closed her eyes against the horrible images that suddenly returned.

Her head ached, and her throat burned. The dryness in her eyes made her want to cry, but no tears would come. She reached up and rubbed at them, amazed by the amount of crud that had built up in the corners. Her hair smelled like smoke, and she could still taste the ash that had been in the air.

"What did I do?" Her voice was nothing more than a scratchy croak. It hurt to talk, but she felt like she deserved that. "I just made things worse, didn't I? If Quinn's really dead this time, Hudson will never speak to me again."

A few hot tears managed to escape one eye.

The door to the room opened, bathing her in bright lights from the hall. She turned her head away, not ready to speak to anyone yet. The door clicked shut, leaving her in near darkness again. Ava let go of the breath she just realized she'd been holding. Someone picked up her hand and gave it a little squeeze.

"Come on, I know you're awake. I saw you move, and I hear your heavy breathing."

"Quinn!" She sat straight up, her body screaming in agony. She groaned as her muscles and joints stretched. "You're not dead!" Ava reached over and touched her friend's face.

Quinn laughed. "Of course I'm not. Thanks to you."

"*I* definitely should be dead. My entire body hurts. My throat is on fire." Ava leaned back against the pillows, her voice cracking as she spoke.

"It's no wonder you're in pain. You were thrown from the car when it rolled. Yet somehow you still managed to pull me from that inferno of a death trap. I literally owe you my life." She squeezed Ava's hand again. "Thank you."

Ava attempted to laugh, but it sounded more like a choking frog. "Like I'd leave you there. We made a pact when we were seven, remember?"

Quinn grinned. "How could I forget? I was betting on that when I sent my boy to the church. I just knew you'd be there that day."

Warmth flooded her as she thought of the precious package Quinn had trusted her with. "Eli is amazing."

"Isn't he?" Quinn's love for the boy emanated from her entire being. "He's the best thing I've ever done."

"He's safe, by the way."

"I know. Hudson's buddy Logan filled me in on a few things once I got out of the emergency room."

"What happened to you, Quinn? Did you get kidnapped? Swept out to sea?"

She shook her head, guilt filling her blue eyes. "I ran away."

"Why would you do *that*? Do you have any idea what it did to Hudson? To me!" The attempt at shouting made her throat ache even more.

"Love makes people do stupid things, I guess. I knew Hudson would never be okay with me marrying the son of a known criminal. But I loved Ricky with all my heart. And life was good for a long time. Until his horrible father got him killed."

A few tears rolled down her face, dripping from her chin.

"I'm so sorry, Quinn. But why did you stay away for so long?"

She sniffed. "Once I learned the truth about the Baron family business, I figured it was better that way. When I met Ricky, I just thought his dad was a drug dealer. Still awful, but nothing like the reality. I figured as long as I didn't get involved in the family business...." She sighed heavily. "Then I had Eli, and Ricky died, and things got really bad. Once I tried to leave, but when Rosario's men found me... well, let's just say I knew leaving wasn't an option. But I had to find a way to save my son. I didn't care what happened to me, but I couldn't let him get to Eli."

"So you left him at the church?"

She nodded. "It wasn't actually me who did it. I made friends with one of the cleaning ladies. She knew what Rosario was like, and she worried about Eli as much as I did. Leaving the baby at the church was my idea. She just carried it out for me. That's why he was in a laundry basket. No one would question her leaving with a load of dry cleaning. I had no idea Hudson had become a cop. That was fate, I suppose, intervening on my behalf."

Hearing Hudson's name brought on a new round of sadness. "At least now he won't hate me even more than he did. You're alive."

Quinn's expression changed instantly, almost like a light switch flipping to the off position. Fear moved into Ava's chest and squeezed at her heart, making breathing even more difficult. She sat forward again, ignoring the aches and pains that assaulted her with the sudden movement.

"What's wrong, Quinn?"

"It's... it's Hudson." Her friend swallowed hard.

"What? What happened?" She yanked at the hoses and wires, trying to free herself.

"He was... hurt." Quinn placed a hand on hers to stop her from pulling at the IV. "Calm down, Ava. You don't need to hurt yourself."

Ava yanked her hand away. "I'm fine! Where is he? I need to see him now." She remembered Rosario shooting at the car behind them. "Was he shot? Please tell me he's okay!"

"He wasn't shot."

Ava paused in her attempts to get out of bed. "Thank goodness for that. I was so worried."

"He wasn't shot, Ava, but he is seriously hurt."

"Quinn! Tell me what happened!" Her heart pounded in her chest, and it became difficult to breathe. "*Please.*" She swung her feet around to stand up, but her legs were far too shaky.

"Only if you promise to calm down and stay put for now. You're not doing you or Hudson any favors if you run out of here and collapse."

Ava dropped back against the pillows, frustrated. The last thing she wanted was to stay in that bed for another second, but Quinn could be bullheadedly stubborn. "Fine. Tell me."

"Let me sit first. My head is still pounding. Doctor says I have a concussion." Quinn pulled the lone chair in the room over to the bedside and sat in it, taking a deep breath. "When he found the crash, he thought we were still in the vehicle. He ran into the flames to try and pull us out."

Ava clapped a hand to her mouth. "Oh God. No."

Quinn held up a hand to stop her from losing it. "His burns are relatively minor compared to what they could have been. Mostly second-degree on his arms and abdomen."

"That's good, then! He'll have some scars, but who cares? He's strong. He'll heal."

Quinn shook her head slowly. "That doesn't seem to be the issue. The doctors are confident that his wounds will eventually heal nicely."

Ava was confused. "Then what?"

"He's unconscious. Has been since we were all brought in yesterday. They have no idea why. He just won't wake up."

Ava let out a little sob. "He's trying to die. He doesn't think you survived."

"Actually, he knows. He found me—and you."

Ava frowned. "Then why isn't he waking up?"

Quinn shrugged and leaned forward, closer to Ava. "When he found us, you... weren't breathing. He performed chest compressions until he passed out. He has no idea you're fine. I've heard a little from Logan about how he pushed you away and all that, but I know he never stopped loving you. It was more obvious than ever when he was there, at the accident, begging you to wake up. If he thinks you're gone, he won't be able to forgive himself."

"No! He can't do that! Not after all I went through to prove to him *you* were still alive!" Panic, a very familiar feeling lately, seized her. "I have to see him. He needs to know."

"I was hoping you'd feel that way." Quinn stood up and pushed her chair back out of the way. "Let me get a nurse to help."

"I don't need help." Ava stood up and promptly got dizzy. She fell back onto the bed. "Okay, maybe I do. Just a little. My head is throbbing."

The door opened again, and a young woman dressed in blue scrubs entered the room. "That's probably the concussion," she said. "You shouldn't be up."

"I need to go." Ava tried standing again and was less dizzy this time, but she got tangled in the wires of the monitors and the hose to the IV machine.

Quinn spoke up. "Would it be possible to get a wheelchair so I can take her to see my brother? She won't settle down until she sees him. I know my best friend."

Ava smiled when she heard Quinn refer to her as her best friend. It had been so many years since she'd heard those words.

"Please? I promise to be good," Ava said, her voice still super scratchy. She reached for a Styrofoam cup with a straw that she'd just noticed sitting on a bedside table and took a long drink of the cold water. "That is so good."

"I don't think you should get up just yet, miss." The nurse looked conflicted, like she wanted to say yes but didn't think she should.

"It might be what he needs to finally wake up. I haven't seen my brother in ten years. I don't want to lose him. Please?" Quinn begged, sounding as worried as she felt. Was Hudson's condition really that serious?

The nurse exhaled. "Okay. Hold on. I'll get a chair."

"Thank you!" Ava and Quinn said at the same time. Totally in tune to each other, just like they always had been. Apparently, neither time nor distance changed some things.

It only took a few minutes for the nurse to return, pushing a wheelchair. As she unhooked Ava's monitor wires and adjusted the intravenous fluid bag to a hook on the wheelchair, she sighed. "I'm such a sucker for love. I hope you can get through to him. You both deserve a happily ever after."

Quinn laughed a little. "You really have no idea. These two have been kindred spirits since the day they first met. And it's all my fault that they aren't already on baby number three with a summer house on the ocean."

Ava's eyes welled up with salt water, a tear rolling down one cheek. "I don't care if he never wants to be with me. He just can't die. I won't let him."

"You can't believe that, Ava. You're the only woman he'll ever love. I know my brother. You didn't see what I saw at the fire. I've been missing ten years, and every ounce of his worry was on you. He's been in love with you his entire life. I should know—I read all his journals like a good kid sister." Quinn smiled and shrugged. "But I would have known it anyway."

The nurse sighed. "This is all so romantic."

Quinn pulled the door open, and the nurse pushed the chair into the hallway. After a short trip in an elevator to the next floor up, they arrived outside Hudson's room.

"Can I be alone with him for a little bit?" Ava asked before they entered.

The nurse and Quinn both nodded.

"Of course, sweetie." Quinn gave her shoulder a slight squeeze. "We'll be right out here if you need us."

Ava pushed at the slightly ajar door, opening it and then letting the nurse wheel her into position beside Hudson's bed. His usually imposing form and personality seemed so small in the sterility of the hospital bed. The nurse slipped from the room, closing the door behind her.

Someone had left the blinds open on the lone window in the room. The streetlights outside bathed him in light. Ava choked back a sob. Hudson's ruddy complexion had turned ashen. Both arms were wrapped in bandages from his shoulder to his wrist on the right and all the way to his fingertips on the left that lay beside his still form. Someone had pulled the sheet and blanket up to cover most of his chest. A few bandage corners peeked out above the white material.

His handsome face had mostly escaped injury. A bandage sat on his forehead, and there was a black streak under his left eye. Otherwise, he appeared to be fine, despite the lack of natural color in his skin.

Wanting to touch him but worried about causing any pain, she carefully placed her hand over the exposed fingers closest to her. At least he still felt warm. She'd been worried for a moment.

"Hudson? It's me, Ava. Quinn says you think I died, but I'm here to tell you I'm totally alive. We need you to wake up. Please. Quinn needs you. *I* need you."

She leaned forward and rested her head on the bed beside him.

"You have a lot of time to make up for. I told you Quinn was alive. You need to be okay. For her. For me too. And don't forget little Eli. He needs to grow up with his uncle Hudson. You're the man in his life now. Don't leave him. Don't leave me."

Her last few words were buried in the tears that finally flowed freely from her smoke-damaged eyes. "I love you, Hudson. I always have, and I always will. Even if you never want to see me again. Just wake up. Please."

She lay there for a long time before finally giving in to the sleep that her injured body demanded.

HUDSON WONDERED IF THE DEAD COULD communicate in his dreams. Like, could an angel visit him that sounded a lot like Ava and try to convince him not to give up on life? It wouldn't make any sense to him at all that God would give him such a gift. Not when he'd been such a dumbass for so long.

Yet Ava's voice was strong in his head. How could that be if she'd died out there beneath those trees? Maybe she was there to show him the way to the other side. He'd read about that a few times.

The morphine drip for his pain kept him pleasantly foggy and in a place he had no desire to leave. Death would even be welcome, knowing he'd never have a chance to apologize to Ava. To confess his feelings and spend the rest of his life making up for all the damage he'd done during the past decade.

He didn't deserve to live.

Not after letting Quinn be alive and in danger for so long without going after her. Not after he'd treated Ava so horribly.

Ava's voice sounded in his mind again. *"I love you, Hudson. I always have, and I always will."*

He dismissed it as wishful thinking. Or a dream. Maybe one of those crossing-the-bridge moments where someone about to die faces all their mistakes.

One of his arms twitched, the skin and muscle rebelling against the damage the fire had done. Stretching a little to calm the fibers, his fingers encountered something soft. He reached out a little more and tried to determine what it was. Opening one eye, despite his best efforts not to, he spotted a mound of dark, wild curls spread across the white blanket covering him.

It couldn't be. He ran his fingertips over a few strands. Maybe?

"Ava?" His throat burned with the effort of making words. The harsh, scratchy sound barely sounded like her name. He tried again. "Have I died and gone to heaven?"

The form half on his bed and half in the wheelchair beside him stirred.

"Ava?" He pushed his vocal cords so hard that time, he nearly gagged.

She lifted her head, sleep mixed with confusion in her beautiful green eyes. As she focused and realized what was happening, she sat straight up.

"Hudson!" Her voice sounded as awful as his. "Oh my God, you're awake!"

He laughed. Or tried to, anyway. "I thought maybe I'd died. I thought you were dead." A sob caught in his throat when he admitted that.

She smiled. "I'm not. Thanks to you."

He shook his head. "I didn't save you. Or Quinn, for that matter. I just made things worse. In every way imaginable." Leaning back against the pillows, he squeezed his eyes shut. "I'm dead. I know it."

Opening one eye and peering at Ava, he still couldn't believe he saw her. She frowned, lines forming on her forehead between her eyes. Those lines had been there since they were kids. He longed to smooth them away with his fingertip, but his body said stay put, so he did.

"Hudson Pierce. You did nothing of the sort. When I needed you, you were there for me. You set aside your own feelings and protected me and Eli."

He grunted. "Yeah, look how that turned out."

"Eli is safe!" The exclamation caused a short coughing fit. When she'd recovered, she took his hand in hers. "It's my fault, not yours. If I hadn't left without telling you, maybe none of this would have happened."

He looked away, hoping to hold back any tears trying to escape. "When I saw that blood in Quinn's room...."

She smiled. "It wasn't ours. The guy shot himself in the leg trying to tackle me. We'd have gotten away if Rosario Baron hadn't sent his entire security team after us."

He frowned. "Rosario Baron. I forgot about him."

She waved a dismissive hand. "Don't worry about

him. He died in the crash. I overheard Logan say the FBI and Homeland Security and a bunch of other agencies were all over his compound and his business."

He reached as far as his wounds would let him and stroked her cheek with his fingertips. Ava leaned into the touch. He didn't deserve one second of her attention. "You were right about Quinn. All these years, you believed. And I didn't. She's alive now because of you."

She slowly stood up, settling herself closer to him on the edge of the bed so he didn't have to reach so far. He appreciated that more than she knew. "You were hurting, Hudson. So much loss so early in your life. No one could blame you. *I* don't blame you."

He ran his fingers along her arm, even that slight motion causing a pain stronger than the morphine could handle. "I was dreaming about you, you know. I think it was the drugs. They made me hear things that weren't true."

She smiled at him, her eyes reflecting something he hadn't seen in a really long time. "Oh? What did the meds make you hear?"

He felt some heat rise in his face. Ava reached over and pressed her palm lightly to his cheek. Ignoring the pain of the motion, he lifted his hand

and placed it over hers. "I thought maybe God sent me an angel who looked like you to take me away. She said—" He swallowed hard against a rise in his emotions. "She said she loved me."

"You silly man!" She laughed as she smoothed some hair back from his forehead. "That wasn't a dream."

He was genuinely confused as he looked at her. Those green eyes he'd always loved so much shone with overtures of feeling and emotion. "I didn't dream it?"

"No! I have always loved you. I never stopped. And no one else could ever take your place. I just hoped that one day you would realize it and forgive me for what happened with Quinn."

He exhaled heavily, the action causing his lungs to ache. He must have inhaled more smoke than he realized. "Quinn...," he said, ignoring the burn in his throat. "I still can't believe she's actually alive. I know it wasn't your fault. I just had no idea how to handle the grief, so I turned it into anger and blame."

Ava's expression turned serious. "She ran away, you know. Quinn."

"She ran away?" He frowned. "Why would she do that?"

"She fell in love with the son of a mobster and

knew you'd never approve, so she left. That mystery boyfriend I told you about? He was the reason. And she was happy, too, but it's not my story to tell. I'll let Quinn do it when she's ready." She swallowed hard and then called out, "Quinn! Come in here!"

His sister opened the door, smiling wide. "You're awake!"

She crossed the room and leaned down to hug Hudson as best as she could around the bandages and wires and IV.

He reached up with his less-injured hand and touched her face. "Where have you been all this time, little sister? They said you were dead." A couple tears escaped his eyes. "I believed them. I shouldn't have, but I did. I didn't know what else to do. I'm so sorry."

"You're sorry?" Quinn sobbed. "Oh, Hudson, I don't know what I was thinking. I was in love, and I knew you'd hate him, and I was just so young—"

"Well, yeah, I would have hated him. Not just because he was a criminal. I would have hated anyone you wanted to date. It's my job as your big brother. You didn't have to run away, though. We could have worked it out."

He'd stopped noticing the tears running down his face at this point. Who cared if the world saw him cry? He'd nearly died, the love of his life nearly died, and he'd just discovered his sister was *not* dead after a decade. That allowed for some crying, in his book.

"I'm so sorry. I hurt you both, and it was incredibly selfish of me." Quinn grabbed some tissues out of the box on the table and handed them around. "I wish you had met Ricky."

"Bring him by. I'd love to have a word with him." Hudson knew he sounded angry, but he also felt a little justified.

Quinn sniffed. "I wish I could, Hud. I really do. But he's... dead."

Hudson's gut clenched hard with his sister's grief. "Dead?"

She shrugged, acceptance and resignation darkening her blue eyes. "His father had him killed. Because of me. And Elijah. That's why I sent Eli to Ava. At least I'd hoped she get him. If anyone could protect my baby, it would be my very best friend."

She let out a sob that shook her entire body. Ava hugged Quinn, and then she hugged Hudson.

She tried to be cautious, but he pulled her in tighter, pressing a kiss to her forehead. "I'm sorry I pushed you away." To Quinn he said, "I'm sorry you didn't think you could trust me."

Quinn let out another round of sobs. "I promise to

never do anything like that again. Especially not now. Elijah needs me. I can't wait to see him again."

He squeezed Quinn's hand with the little bit of strength he could muster. "Soon. He's safe. And I have a lot of explaining to do to a lot of people when I get out of here."

"Will you be in big trouble with your job?" Quinn asked.

Hudson shrugged. "My captain knows where I am, and he told me to protect Eli, so I'll probably be fine in that respect. But I'm pretty sure I've pissed off a lot of people over the years with my angry-recluse personality."

Knowing his sister had intentionally left stirred a whole other bunch of emotions he didn't feel prepared to deal with at the moment.

He tugged lightly on one of Ava's curls. "You kept your faith all these years while I just couldn't. Because of you, everything I thought I'd never have is possible again."

Ava tilted her head to the side slightly, obvious questions in her eyes. "Everything?"

"Quinn's alive. You're alive. And even if I never vocalized the thoughts, my heart has always known."

"Oh?" She leaned in a little closer. He could smell the smoke in her hair, and to him, it was a glorious smell—it meant she'd survived. "What has your heart always known?"

"It knew I never stopped loving you and that I hoped to one day do this again." With his less-injured hand, Hudson pulled Ava in closer and pressed a soft kiss to her lips. "I love you, Ava Taft. And I know I have a lot of time to make up for, but I want to spend every day from now on proving it to you and making up for the way I treated you."

"You have nothing to prove and nothing to make up for." She kissed him again. "I just think maybe it's time we leave the past in the past and move forward. I've always been a sucker for a happily ever after."

"Then your wish shall be my command. You know, once I get out of this hospital bed."

Ava laughed—a more beautiful sound he'd never heard. "Let's repeat this conversation when you aren't completely high on pain meds."

He took her hand in his. "No need to. I'm perfectly sober at the moment. I love you, Ava, and I will never stop. We deserve our happily ever after, and I promise you it'll be worth it."

She leaned in once more, and he kissed her with a thousand promises of all the tomorrows they would share. Everything finally felt at peace in the world.

He turned to his sister. "You and I have some

things to talk about. I want to know everything that's happened since you left."

Quinn nodded. "Of course. Once I get settled. I need to find somewhere for me and Eli—"

"You'll both stay with me. I have a few bullet holes to patch and a broken window or two to fix, but my home is your home."

His sister looked horrified. "Bullet holes?"

Ava chuckled. "We have a lot to catch up on, my beautiful friend."

Hudson nodded. "So much. But now we have all the time in the world to do so. I love you both. Not in the same way, of course. That would really get me in trouble with my job."

Ava and Quinn started laughing at the same time. "That's the brother I've missed for so long," Quinn said.

The nurse poked her head in around the door. "I think it's time for all three of you to get some rest. Back to your rooms, girls."

Ava shook her head. "I don't want to leave."

He squeezed her hand. "Once we're out of here, we will never have to be apart again."

"Is that a promise?" she asked.

"A vow." Hudson pulled her in for one more kiss. "I love you, Ava. Marry me? You know, once I heal, and the doctors tell me they have successfully removed my head from my hind end where it's been firmly embedded for a decade?"

"Of course, you stubborn man. It's only ever been you. I just had to wait for you to figure it out."

EPILOGUE

 Quinn wrapped her in a tight hug. "I can't believe this day has finally arrived!"

Ava laughed. "*You* can't believe it?"

Quinn smoothed out a couple of the ringlets framing Ava's face, setting them into place. "I honestly believed that when I left, you and Hudson would get married and have each other. It never occurred to me that he would push you away. Not when he'd been in love with you for most of his life."

Ava's grandmother had insisted she carry two antique handkerchiefs that had belonged to *her* mother tucked into the bodice of her gown. She'd thought the idea to be ridiculous at the time, but now it made perfect sense. Ava fished one out and dabbed at her eyes. "It doesn't matter anymore, Quinn. The last year and a half have been absolutely perfect. We've rediscovered our love as adults. It almost feels like a dream. In a few minutes, we'll be husband and wife and spend the rest of our lives making up for that time we lost."

"Hi, Auntie Awa." Elijah, her soon-to-be nephew, toddled over, looking absolutely adorable in his little linen suit. At nearly two, he spoke incredibly well but still had some words to work on, like her name.

She ruffled his hair. "You look very handsome, little man."

"You wook hansand too." He gave her a drooly grin.

To Quinn she said, "I couldn't love him more if he were my own child. Thank you for trusting me with him when you did."

"There's no one else I would have except for you and my brother. I knew you'd keep him safe no matter what."

She heard some music begin to play outside the tent. One of the flaps opened. "You about ready to get hitched, bestie? The weather's perfect for a wedding."

Ava nodded. "I'm beyond ready."

"Eli and I will lead the way." Quinn gave her a kiss on the cheek before stepping out of the tent.

Pachelbel's "Canon in D" played as Ava and her father left the tent as well. Hudson's already amazing backyard had been turned into a fairy-tale garden. The smell of honeysuckle wafted through the air as decorations waved lightly in the breeze. Candles in Mason jars lit a path through the dusk straight to the edge of the pond where Pastor Barrett stood with Hudson.

When they made eye contact, he mouthed, "I love you."

Unable to control the wash of love she felt, Ava let her tears fall as she waited for Eli to carry the rings down the lit path.

Quinn walked behind him, dropping white rose petals as she walked. All of a sudden, Eli spotted Hudson and yelled, "Uncle Husson!" before tossing the pillow with the rings attached and taking off in a sprint the rest of the way to where Hudson stood. "Wook!" He pointed at Ava. "Auntie Awa is so pwetty!"

"She sure is, buddy." Hudson wiped at his own eyes as he turned all his attention on her.

As the candles flickered and the sun set behind the trees and dunes, Ava had never felt so happy in her life.

She handed her bouquet to Quinn and took

Hudson's outstretched hands in hers. She barely noticed the burn scars anymore. He'd healed even more cleanly than the doctors had predicted.

"I do," Hudson said. "Forever."

Pastor Barrett laughed. "I think you got a little ahead of me, son."

Hudson shook his head. "Actually, with all due respect, sir, I'm way behind on this one." To Ava he said, "I love you. And I promise to cherish you and protect you always. Thank you for never giving up on me."

"I love you too." She smiled through her tears. "I promise to also cherish and protect you always. And I will *never* give up on us."

He pulled her close, wrapping his arms around her, and kissed her with a decade's worth of love and emotion.

"I guess I'm not actually needed here today!" Pastor Barrett said, laughing. "But, just for luck—by the power vested in me by the state of North Carolina and the good Lord, I now pronounce you husband and wife. May no man put asunder what the Lord has created."

"I love you," Hudson murmured against her lips.

Ava kissed him once more. "And I love you. Always."

ACKNOWLEDGMENTS

I wrote my very first novel back in 1999. I was a lab tech in a chemical engineering research lab. My days were spent watching reactions run for six hours, taking temperature and pH measurements every hour. I sat on my stool with a yellow legal pad and wrote a serial killer murder mystery by hand. At night I sat at my computer and typed the words of the day into a digital manuscript. I never expected, twenty-two years later, to have written nearly twenty novels, novellas, and short stories. I definitely had no expectation of publication. Having loyal readers? Nope.

Over the years, so many people have supported me in the writing process. I could never name them all individually. A huge thank-you to my husband for always believing in me. Deadlines make me cranky, but he rides it out perfectly, sometimes tossing chocolate or SweetTarts at me.

Allie Kincheloe, if you hadn't taken a chance on a completely unknown writer who could never seem to use a comma appropriately, I wouldn't be writing this thank-you. Your editing skills and your friendship have meant the world to me. So many things have happened since we first met in 2015, both in publishing and our personal lives, that I couldn't imagine having gone through without your support.

To Becky Johnson and all the amazing editors and staff of Hot Tree Publishing, you are all amazing. You take my stories and make them into beautiful works of art. Your dedication to authors and publishing is unmatched in my experience.

Thank you, Booksmith Designs, for the most beautiful cover. You've created a visual brand for my novels that is absolutely perfect.

Readers, thank you most of all. Without you, my stories would remain secrets. You read them, love them, share them, and make me want to keep writing. For that, I am eternally grateful.

ABOUT THE AUTHOR

Science teacher by day, writer and baseball mom by night, Carolyn LaRoche lives near the ocean with her husband, two boys, rescue puppy, and four cats. She loves crocheting, books, food videos and trying new recipes.

Join Carolyn's newsletter:

WWW.CAROLYNLAROCHE.WORDPRESS.COM

Carolyn would love to hear from you directly too. Please feel free to email her at CAROLYN LAROCHEAUTHOR@YAHOO.COM or check out her website WWW.CAROLYNLAROCHE.WORD-PRESS.COM for updates.

ABOUT THE PUBLISHER

Hot Tree Publishing loves love. Publishing adult romantic fiction, HTPubs are all about diverse reads featuring heroes and heroines to swoon over. Since opening in 2015, HTPubs have published more than 300 titles across the wide and diverse range of romantic genres. If you're chasing a happily ever after in your favourite subgenre, HTPubs have you covered.

Interested in discovering more amazing reads brought to you by Hot Tree Publishing? Head over to the website for information:

WWW.HOTTREEPUBLISHING.COM